FOOTPRINTS
IN THE DUST

L.E. Hutchinson

L.E. HUTCHINSON

On the Cover: Norman S. Lowery, U.S. Army Retired. 2017.

Monday Creek Publishing

Ohio USA

ISBN-10: 0692863311
ISBN-13: 978-0692863312

DEDICATION

To my three daughters, Kathy, Serena, and Sandy, who gave me support, encouragement, and most of all, love.

To my sisters-in-law, Joan and Nancy, who listened to me, cheered me on and helped to inspire me.

To Anne for keeping me in her prayers.

And, to Gina, for all of her help and lifting me up when I needed it most.

Thank you all!

1 Jon 4:8 "God is love."

ACKNOWLEDGMENTS

Special thanks to Norman S. Lowery (cover photograph) who served in the United States Army, December 1962 to February 1983: 1SG, First Sargent E-8, Field Artillery, Airborne Ranger, Military Police, Air Department Marshal, Drill Sargent, and Army Recruiter. Lowery served in Government Service, Security Police, and as a Morgan County Deputy Sheriff. He retired from Ohio University, Athens, Ohio, Resident Hall Director. Lowery is an active solider in the Civil War reenactment scenes throughout Ohio.

Thanks to the Putnam County Courthouse, Ottawa, Ohio, for their expertise in obtaining Civil War documents.

Chapter One
Putnam County, Ohio 1860

The horse drawn buckboard wagon came to a slow halt in front of McClure's General Store in Kalida. The young man driving the team was tan from working in the fields under the hot summer sun, his blue eyes squinting from too much sunlight.

Suddenly a young lady walked out of the general store. The young man leaped down from the wagon and loose dirt scattered when his dusty boots touched the ground. He tied the horses to the hitching post and stepped up onto the porch to stand next to the girl.

Nervously he combed his fingers through his light blond hair and he pulled a handkerchief from his pants pocket to wipe the sweat from his face.

The young woman wore a brown cotton prairie dress and homemade sunbonnet with a wide brim that hid her face. She looked up at him through shy brown eyes and just a hint of a smile on her lips as her heart beat rapidly. He made her nervous and excited at the same time. She liked being near him. Quickly she looked down at the rough plank porch floor. They knew they were destined to one day be together.

"It's a mighty hot day!" He again wiped the sweat from his face. "How's your Mama?" He stammered for the words as he looked on and saw Mrs. Truby. She was sitting on the bench under a large shade tree just beyond the store where their horse and buggy were tied up.

"All is well. Mama waits for me yonder." She hurriedly stepped down off the porch carrying a few purchased items in a basket.

The tall handsome young man waved to Mrs. Truby and she nodded her head in acknowledgement. A welcome gentle breeze blew across his sunburned face as he stood there affectionately watching Adaline as she walked away.

In a flash, he jumped down from the porch and raced toward Adaline and Mrs. Truby.

He called out, "Let me help you!" He ran to catch up with Adaline.

He helped Mrs. Truby up into the buggy and handed her the horse's reins, then quickly ran around to where Adaline stood waiting with basket in hand. He held her arm to steady her as she climbed up onto the seat. As he handed her the basket she looked into his loving eyes.

"Ye be comin' to church on Sunday?" Mrs. Truby questioned him in her thick German accent.

"Ain't no worry about that," said the young man with a twinkle in his eyes. "I just consider myself lucky to sit with you. If you don't mind?"

"Tis always pleasin' to see ye there," said Mrs. Truby. Adaline glanced at the young man and smiled.

"You be careful going home," S.W. cautioned.

"No need to worry 'bout us," said Mrs. Truby as she took control of the reins to head the horse towards home.

S.W. turned around and slowly walked back to the store. The nineteen-year-old stood on the porch dreaming and thinking about Adaline.

Adaline who was sixteen and her older sister Betsy, along with her brother, Samuel, who was the oldest, and their mother, Mrs. Truby, worked hard to keep their small farm going. The Truby family had journeyed from New York to the northwestern part of Ohio. They settled first in Independence and then moved onto Franconia, Ohio. It was a hard life since Adaline's father had died, leaving Samuel the responsibility of caring for the family.

As S.W. stood on the porch he said a silent prayer, "Please Lord, take care of Adaline and her family."

"If ye's done dreamin' 'bout that purdy gal, I could get ye

what ye come after!" S.W. could hear Mr. McClure, the store owner, bellowing from inside the store. Then after some hesitation, Mr. McClure asked, "Ye be a wantin' to marry her?"

"I'm thinking about it," S.W. answered as he entered the store.

Mr. McClure grinned. He knew that S.W came from a loving family who gained their strength from their Bible based faith and that he was a hard-working young man.

"Well, young'un, do ye need supplies?"

The smell of tobacco, spices, and coffee drifted in the air as S.W. entered the general store. Cast iron pots, skillets, and pans were hanging on the walls along with brooms, buckets, ropes, washboards and even cowbells. Hats, shoes and boots were for sale too. Leather bags, canteens, combs, ribbons, bows, and wax candles were laid out on the counter near where Mr. McClure stood. Coal oil lamps were on a shelf behind him.

S.W. handed the big burly man his supply list. Mr. McClure's dirty muslin cloth apron was barely sufficient to cover his stomach and tie in the back. S.W. liked Mr. McClure, as did most folks. He was a good judge of character and an honest businessman. He knew all the folks who came to his store by their first names as well as their children's names.

"Well, young'un, ye been thinkin' any 'bout the Lincoln-Douglas debate?"

"No, I been too busy. I don't have time to keep up on gossip," said S.W. as he chewed on a broom straw and waited on Mr. McClure to fill the order.

"Ye do know that Lincoln's a candidate for president? That ain't no gossip! A peddler come by a day or two ago, journeyed in from Illinois. He said Lincoln's a gainin' a good reputation and he delivers a mighty good speech. There's been talk 'bout southern states secedin' from the Union, and the South wants to expand slavery into the western territories."

"Well, Mr. McClure, I don't claim to know much about politics. I reckon you keep up with all the latest news and I'll take your word for it. If it comes to defending the North then I'll have to join up, but I don't want to think of it just yet." S.W. sighed and then said, "I best get the wagon loaded and move on down the road."

"Oh, say, the peddler left some Bowie knives and a couple of rifles. Ye better take a look. There might come a day when ye need some weapons on that farm. One is a French-foldin' knife. Ye might take a real likin' to that one." Mr. McClure had the knack for selling and confidence resonated in his voice, but S.W. wasn't buying.

"No thanks. I got all the weapons I need and I trust in the Lord for my protection."

"I know ye is a good lad," said Mr. McClure as he helped lift the last crate for S.W. to place in the wagon.

Just as S.W. was arranging the wooden crates in the back of the buckboard wagon he noticed a covered wagon coming in from the east trail. The covered wagon slowly rolled to a stop under the shade tree at the corner of the store. A huge man slid down from the wagon seat and tied the horses to the hitching post.

S.W. was moving the wooden crates around in the back of his wagon as the man stepped up onto the porch where Mr. McClure was swishing an old broom across the floor. Mr. McClure bid S.W. farewell before speaking to the stranger.

"What can I do for ye?" Mr. McClure asked the huge man. The man's clothes were well worn and soiled. A strong body odor made it difficult to stand near the man.

"Well, I'm a headed north on into Canada. I'm in need of a few things to tide me over on the trip thar. Since ya got this store and all, I reckoned maybe ya might be interested in tradin' fer some hides and fur." The man leaned over the porch railing and spit tobacco juice on the ground.

"I reckon I can take a look at what ye got," Mr. McClure told the man and he followed him to the back of his covered wagon.

S.W. had turned his wagon around and was heading for home when he took one more look back at the store before getting out of sight. He saw Mr. McClure fall to the ground and the huge man running inside the store. S.W. turned his wagon around and went back. However, when S.W. got to the store, the huge man was back in his wagon and rapidly heading out of town on the old north trail going towards Toledo.

S.W. found Mr. McClure to be barely conscious after being struck on the head with a wooden club. S.W. knelt on the ground to help Mr. McClure get up.

"Mr. McClure, I'm getting you to the doctor. Do you hear me? Mr. McClure, do you hear me?" S.W. asked and then added in a low tone, "I think you're the one who needs to keep a weapon handy."

Mr. McClure moaned in pain as blood trickled down his forehead. S.W. helped Mr. McClure get in the back of the wagon and then he ran to lock up the store.

S.W. stopped the wagon in front of the doctor's office and two men who were standing in the street helped to get Mr. McClure inside. The two men went immediately to notify the sheriff of the attack and robbery.

Once S.W. knew that Mr. McClure was going to be alright, he went home to the farm and conveyed the details of the robbery to Oliver. Oliver was S.W.'s oldest brother. Oliver was a muscled and toughened young man with blond hair and bright blue eyes. He was generally mild tempered, not to be ruled out that he could easily fend for himself and protect the family if need be. Oliver had taken charge of managing the family farm following the death of their grandfather in 1852.

Their parents had died early on in 1847 and that was when their grandfather had rescued the farm and the children: Amy Ann, Gilbert, Charlotte, S.W., Oliver, and Hannah, the oldest girl.

S.W. continued to explain what had happened. "The thief got away with a gunnysack full of food and some other items. I think he took a little money too. He surely seemed like an odd sort of fella. He was big, dirty, and he stunk to high heaven. I reckon he won't be back around these parts."

"Well, you're home safe and McClure is going to be fine. It could have been worse. We can look in on McClure tomorrow," said Oliver as he jumped down from the porch of the old log house.

Fourteen-year-old Gilbert rushed out to join them in helping to unload the wagon. Gilbert was a rambunctious young lad who was always ready for excitement.

"I heard you talkin' 'bout Mr. McClure gettin' robbed. Is he alright?"

"He's spending the night at the Doc's house. He'll be fine in the morning," S.W. replied.

"Oh my goodness, who would want to hurt Mr. McClure? I do hope that thief isn't still around these parts!" Charlotte sounded upset as she came outside and stood on the porch. Charlotte's blond hair was pulled into one long braid going right down the middle of her back. Her fair skin was unblemished except for a few freckles on her arms. Her eyes were the same bright blue as her brothers'. She wore a dark green prairie styled dress with white high waist apron which made her look older than seventeen.

"Charlotte, there's no need to worry yourself about it. The Sheriff has been notified and folks in town will be on the lookout for the robber if he comes back around," Oliver confirmed their safety.

"Well, if he comes 'round here I'll take a club to his head!" Gilbert raised his voice and his blue eyes wide open as he alluded to being fearless.

"Gilbert, you don't need to take a club to anybody," S.W. said as he annoyingly glanced at Gilbert.

"Now, Charlotte, what's for supper?" S.W. inquired.

"Bean soup, biscuits, and salt pork," answered Charlotte.

"Ahhh, I'm gettin' tired of beans," Gilbert complained.

"You better quit your belly achin' or I won't bake that gingerbread you like so much." Charlotte patted Gilbert on his head and mussed up his thick blond hair.

"Ahhh, Sis, you're always treatin' me like a baby. I'm fourteen now! I'm even old enough to go off to war if I wanna," Gilbert argued defensively.

Charlotte quickly remarked, "Why, who's been talking to you about war? You will have no part of killing! Do you hear me, Gilbert?"

S.W. spoke up before young Gilbert had a chance to respond. "You been hanging out over at the Donaldsons' place?"

Gilbert sheepishly answered, "Their Pa got the latest newspaper from Kalida. The front page was all 'bout Lincoln runnin' for president and...

"Gilbert, I will not hear another word of it!" Charlotte interrupted him. "You go and draw a bucket of water from the well so we can wash up for supper."

Gilbert stomped out the back door and headed toward the well. He lifted the heavy wooden cover from the top of the well and fastened the bucket to the rope. Gilbert had no trouble cranking the large handle to turn the wooden beam as the bucket lowered into the water.

"Crank a little faster and draw another bucket for the house," said Oliver as he stood waiting with a wash pan in his hands.

"Ahhh, you're always bossin' me 'round," Gilbert complained.

Gilbert filled the wash pan with water and Oliver walked to the back porch and placed the wash pan on an old bench. S.W. came out on the porch to clean up too.

"That Gilbert worries me," S.W. stated as he hung the muslin towel on a wooden peg.

Oliver finished drying his face and hands before speaking.

"Well, everyone is talking about the Lincoln-Douglas debates. In that speech that Lincoln gave last year in New York City, he clearly denounced slavery."

"So what are you saying?" S.W. looked puzzled.

"I'm getting a little worried myself and I know Gilbert is probably worried too." Oliver saw Gilbert coming toward the house with a bucket of water and nothing more was said.

As S.W. and Oliver stood on the back porch they could clearly see company coming up the lane. S.W yelled through the kitchen door to Charlotte and Amy Ann to come outside as a buggy was fast approaching.

Charlotte recognized the chestnut colored horse and enclosed buggy. Charlotte and Amy Ann quickly ran out into the yard to greet their company.

"Oh, Aunt Sarah, you're just in time to eat with us! Henry, you can join us too!" Amy Ann was excited to have company. The girls hugged Aunt Sarah and then walked arm-in-arm with her to the house.

"Oh, girls, I can't stay long. And as for Henry he can wait on the back porch. I came to see if there is anything you need," she said as they walked together.

How poor old Henry managed to put up with Aunt Sarah for all these years was beyond anyone's imagination. Henry had been a dedicated servant for Aunt Sarah and her family. No one knew exactly for how long except that he traveled from

East Liverpool with the family when they came to live in Putnam County. Aunt Sarah called him her servant, not a slave, and she made sure people knew that. She adamantly denied that he came from the slave auction house in Wheeling, Virginia[1] . Even if no one asked, she still clarified that Henry was not a slave.

"Yes, Aunt Sarah, do hurry!" said Charlotte.

"Yes, hurry," said Amy Ann.

Amy Ann's light blond hair was parted in the middle and braided in two long braids. Her printed plum colored calico dress touched just above her ankles showing her black high-, button shoes as she went up the steps.

"Gilbert, go with Henry and help take the horse out back where there is shade and hurry back so we can eat together," Charlotte directed Gilbert.

"There you go again, bossin' me 'round!" Gilbert complained.

Then Gilbert saw Aunt Sarah and he calmly added, "Oh, hello Aunt Sarah. What brings you out here?"

Aunt Sarah didn't have a chance to answer Gilbert because Charlotte and Amy Ann rushed her inside the old log house.

"Here, Aunt Sarah, you can sit here." Amy Ann dragged the chair across the rough wooden floor to the end of the table.

---

[1] June 20, 1863, West Virginia became the Country's 35th State.

Just then Oliver, S.W., and Gilbert entered through the backdoor and sat down at the table. They sat in the same seat at every meal except for tonight. They seemed to have forgotten their places and sat in different seats. Aunt Sarah had a way of making them nervous as she was keen on manners and tried her best to keep up on all the local social events.

"Here, let me take your bonnet. I'll hang it up over here on the wall for you... to keep it clean." S.W. offered with an outstretched hand.

She seemed to be inspecting his hands to see if they were indeed clean before handing it to him. She smiled politely as she handed over her bonnet.

Aunt Sarah was wearing a summery yellow dress with a delicate floral pattern. She looked much older than forty-eight years. Her dark hair was parted in the middle of her head and tightly pulled back into a fashionable bun.

S.W. sat back down and said, "Aunt Sarah, please join us in prayer. Let us all join hands."

Before she had a chance to reply, Amy Ann grabbed her hand on the right side and S.W. sitting to the left of her, reached out and grasped her hand tightly. S.W. quickly said a prayer and then Charlotte ladled out the bean soup from the kettle. The biscuits were passed around the table along with the butter and a platter of salt pork. Charlotte passed around a pitcher of sassafras tea to pour into the brown glazed mugs.

"Oh, I am so glad you are using the Rockingham Ware!" Aunt Sarah boldly stated.

Charlotte quickly replied, "Yes, and thank you so much for the gifts. We truly enjoy the new pottery."

The boys raised their eyebrows and looked at one another with disdain, but Aunt Sarah never noticed.

"I'm so glad none of it was broken when it was shipped. You know, children, it was shipped from East Liverpool, to Cincinnati by riverboat," she smiled, paused, and continued talking. "I really must take the girls with me someday to my hometown of East Liverpool. It is such a busy river town. You do know that East Liverpool produces half of our country's Yellow Ware and Rockingham Ware, not to mention all the doorknobs come from The Riverside Knob Works," she announced this with great pride in her voice. She continued speaking, "Oh, and I must take the girls to visit Pittsburgh. It's such a big city now. Oh, but with all this talk of the Southern

Rebellion... perhaps I will never see East Liverpool again." Her voice sounded sorrowful as she dabbed her eyes with the towel.

Gilbert was wide-eyed and intently listening. He sat there contemplating the idea of fancy doorknobs.

"Doorknobs? Why do folks want fancy doorknobs?" Gilbert questioned. "What's wrong with wooden handles and metal latches and leather straps?"

Amy Ann joined in the conversation. "Really? Gilbert, some people just like fancy things in their homes. I wish we had some fancy things. I can just imagine a grand house with glass or porcelain doorknobs. I can see myself living in just such a place!"

"Of course you do, sweet girl. It is so hard for a young girl growing up in this part of the country," Aunt Sarah sympathized with her.

Charlotte passed the butter to Aunt Sarah. "Please, have some butter with your biscuit. Would you like some honey?"

"Thank you." Aunt Sarah continued to spread a small amount of butter over the biscuit and delicately drizzled honey over it with a spoon.

"I feel like you are my own children. Your Mama meant so much to me. The poor dear... oh, how I do miss my sister." She lowered her head and patted the towel to her eyes.

"Why don't you have your own children?" Gilbert blurted out.

"Gilbert, that will be enough," demanded his big brother Oliver. "Aunt Sarah has been very generous to us since Pappy and Mama died. Gilbert, you best mind your manners."

"That is quite alright Oliver. Gilbert is just a lad. I really must be leaving now. And please let me know if you need anything. I will have it promptly delivered." She excused herself from the table.

They all stood up to bid her a good-day and wish her a safe trip home. Gilbert suddenly had to inform her of the recent robbery at McClure's General Store before allowing her to leave.

"Oh, my goodness, I do hope Mr. McClure is alright," Aunt Sarah gasped.

"It was just a bump on the head. He's at the Doc's for the night," Gilbert impulsively blurted out.

"Oh, I certainly hope the culprit gets caught!" Aunt Sarah loudly declared. "Mr. McClure is just too trusting of strangers. You just can't trust anyone these days." Aunt Sarah paused and scratched her head. "Why that just makes me think of that strange character we passed on the way over here." Aunt Sarah straightened her dress and proceeded toward the door and then she suddenly stopped and turned around to face everyone. "Why, he was a big burly looking man driving a covered wagon. He nearly ran us off the road he was in such a hurry!" Aunt Sarah paused again and then stated, "Why, you don't suppose he was the robber?" Aunt Sarah gasped as it dawned on her.

"Exactly where did you see this covered wagon? Was it headed north?" S.W. inquired.

"Well, let me think on it. It was where the road forks and the old road goes north to Toledo. Oh, my, I just don't know which way he went. He was going so fast," Aunt Sarah shook her head in confusion.

"Well, Aunt Sarah, I figure he took the old stagecoach road north and he is long gone. No need to worry, but I can escort you back into town if you like." S.W. offered.

"No thank you. Henry and I will be fine. I'm sure the robber hasn't lingered. Only a fool would linger."

Charlotte jumped up, handed Aunt Sarah her bonnet, then walked out with her. Amy Ann followed fast behind them.

"Must you go so soon, Aunt Sarah?" Amy Ann pleaded for her to stay.

Aunt Sarah was busy making a bow with the strings on her bonnet and didn't reply as she was still quite shaken from the thoughts of having passed the robber on the road.

Henry was sitting on the back porch when they came out. He had heard them talking about the robbery and quickly stated, "I'll be on the lookout Little Missy. Don't you worry none." He tipped his hat to the girls and hurriedly went to get the horse and buggy.

Aunt Sarah stood on the porch waiting for Henry to bring the buggy around and the girls promptly hugged and kissed her goodbye. They waved to her as she was leaving and watched until the buggy was out of sight.

Henry safely delivered Aunt Sarah back to her home and the thief who robbed and injured Mr. McClure wasn't seen or heard from again.

Chapter Two
Evening Comes and a New Day Begins

*A*unt Sarah had gone, but there was still work to be done before retiring for the night. Charlotte stood in the kitchen looking at the wood stove and thinking about the gingerbread she planned on making before ending her day.

The four-burner wood stove had an oven located underneath for baking and a water reservoir above to keep water hot at all times. A stack of firewood was always needed in the kitchen and on the back porch.

S.W laid a bundle of firewood beside the stove and said he would be back soon as he was going over to visit Adaline's brother, Samuel.

"I'll mix up some gingerbread while you're gone," Charlotte announced.

"Save some for me!" S.W. responded as he hurried out the backdoor.

"I can't make any promises!" Charlotte shouted to him.

S.W. and Samuel worked together at the sawmill located on the Truby property and over time they had acquired some regular customers. S.W. hoped that Samuel would be agreeable to loading the lumber tonight and making the delivery to the cabinetmaker early in the morning.

It was only a short distance to the Truby place. The horses whinnied softly when they neared the farm. As the wagon wheels turned, dust rose in the air and settled back down on the narrow winding road. S.W. pulled back on the long leather reins as the horses passed the bend in the road and he guided the team to a slow stop in front of the small white farmhouse.

Mrs. Truby cheerfully smiled at S.W. as she was on her way to the barn to do the milking. S.W. jumped down from the wagon and tied the reins to a post near the house. He knocked on the front door and Samuel called out for him to come in.

Samuel was a tall, handsome young man in his early twenties. He was taller than S.W. and a bit more rugged. When S.W. entered the house, Betsy was cleaning off the table as Samuel had just finished eating his supper. Adaline was nowhere in sight.

"Can I get ye somethin' to eat?" asked Betsy.

"Betsy was a matter-of-fact, straight forward kind of gal, but that was alright because women folk had to take care of themselves in this part of the country," S.W. thought to himself.

Betsy was short, of medium build with dark curly hair and always a sparkle in her eyes. She was friendly, sometimes too friendly. S.W. thought she might have her sights set on him. Regardless of what he thought, she was Adaline's sister and he needed to keep mannerly and at a distance.

"Oh, no thank you. I just ate with the folks. Everything sure smells good," replied S.W.

"Well... are ye sure ye wouldn't be interested in a bite of bread puddin'?" Betsy tried to persuade him and then added, "Tis still nice and warm." S.W. got a whiff of cinnamon and raisins from the hot pudding as Betsy removed it from the oven.

"Oh, no thank you." S.W. smiled graciously.

"What brings ye this way?" Samuel questioned.

"I was thinking we could load the wagon tonight instead of in the morning so we can leave early. It is a bit of a trip to Ottawa." S.W. made a reasonable suggestion.

Samuel agreed, "Well... ye is right 'bout that. Let's get a move on. It will be dark soon."

S.W. followed Samuel to the back of the house. It was to his surprise to find Adaline working in the fenced-in-garden. Tall colorful hollyhock flowers were growing along the white picket fence. The sun was slowly moving across the western horizon and sundown would be a welcome end to a long hot day.

"Adaline! I wondered where you were!" He felt drawn to her, but the words he wanted to say would not come forth.

"Tis good to see ye again," she said and smiled at him.

The evening sun was shining in her face and beads of perspiration formed on her forehead. Her white apron was tied tightly around her waist which drew S.W.'s attention to her womanly figure. Adaline's dark waist-length hair was braided and coiled around her face and pinned atop her head. The sunbonnet was tied around her neck and loosely draped down her back. The soft delicate nape of her neck induced an arousing desire in him. He was momentarily lost in shameful thoughts. Quickly he regained his composure when Samuel called from a distance.

"S.W.! Hurry! Darkness will be upon us!"

"I'll see you later Adaline," said S.W. as he ran fast to catch up with Samuel.

Samuel was sitting on the wagon seat holding the reins and impatiently waiting. S.W. climbed up onto the wagon seat. The large work horses were slow moving. The clopping of the horse's heavy hooves made a rhythmic sound on the road. The only other sounds on this hot summer evening were the calling of a bird named a Bob White and the distant screeching of a night owl on the hunt for food.

Just a few feet before they reached the sawmill the horses

became startled and began striking the ground with their hooves. A reddish brown, copper colored snake slithered across the dirt road and into the tall weeds.

"It's a copperhead! Must've been about three feet long!" Samuel said as he struggled to keep control of the horses.

"Plenty more where he came from. Best keep an eye out and have the axe ready while we load," S.W. said. "More of those slithering devils could be lurking in the planks."

The two young men worked fast and were finished loading the wagon just before sundown.

Adaline was sitting on the front porch in a rocking chair enjoying the cool night air when S.W and Samuel got back to the house. Samuel went around to the back porch to clean up. S.W. sat down on the front porch steps to rest for a few minutes before going home.

"Adaline," he spoke very softly. "Not a day goes by that I don't think of you. I don't want to make promises that I can't keep. If you could just give me some time to prove myself then we could have our own little place and be together forever." He got up and kissed her on the cheek, jumped off the porch and ran home.

Adaline was pleasantly surprised and continued to gently rock in the chair dreaming of S.W. when her Mama called from inside the house.

"Adaline! Tis time to come in the house now and clean

up."

S.W. got back home in time to eat some of the nice warm gingerbread that Charlotte had made, but he had trouble falling asleep that night as he couldn't keep his mind off Adaline.

The next morning S.W was up before sunrise getting ready for the journey to Ottawa. He hurried out of the house and down the road. His long legs swiftly carried him to be with young Adaline.

Samuel was waiting on the porch. "Come on in the house and get somethin' to eat before we go."

Mrs. Truby was pouring the boiling hot coffee into cups with saucers to let it cool.

"S.W., would ye mind sayin' the prayer this mornin'?" Mrs. Truby asked.

Mrs. Truby took her seat at the table and they bowed their heads in prayer and S.W. recited a blessing over the food.

"Tis nice to have a new voice at our table," said Mrs. Truby.

S.W and Samuel finished eating and excused themselves from the table. They walked outside to round up the horses and hitch up the wagon.

Mrs. Truby, Betsy, and Adaline walked out onto the front porch to see them off. "God bless," said Mrs. Truby.

S.W. gently tapped the reins on the horse's hind quarters

and called out, "Giddy-up!"

Adaline and Betsy waved goodbye and watched until the wagon was out of sight.

Chapter Three
Early August 1860
Unexpected Encounters

It was slow traveling as the horses pulled the heavy load. They needed to stop along the way to rest and water the horses. After arriving in Ottawa, Samuel and S.W. unloaded the lumber at the cabinetmaker's shop, collected their pay, then left the team at the livery stable. As they walked down the dirt street, they could hear the train whistle in the distance.

"Well, here comes the mornin' train," said Samuel. The train whistle blew two more times as it slowed to a stop in front of the hotel depot. Eight passengers departed from the coach: three young women, an older lady and gentleman with a small boy, and two well-dressed men carrying expensive tailor-made suit coats over their arms.

The three young women waited on the depot platform for the porter to deliver their bags. When S.W. and Samuel drew nearer they realized that the young women were also going to the hotel. Samuel lagged behind to hold open the hotel entrance door for the women.

"Ladies, allow us to help with those bags," offered Samuel. He was smiling and his brown eyes sparkled with teasing enticement. His tanned muscular body had the power to attract their attention.

"Why, thank you very much," said one of the young women. She was wearing a dark blue dress with a white crocheted collar and crocheted edging on the sleeves. She clutched a black leather drawstring purse in one hand and a white parasol in the other. Her black hair was neatly pulled back under her bonnet and flowing down over her shoulders. Samuel was quite taken by her beauty. He and S.W picked up the bags and followed the ladies to the desk to register.

The hotel clerk stood at attention when the young lady approached. He was a tall thin man with wire-rimmed glasses.

"How can I help you?" asked the clerk.

"Well, kind sir, we are in need of a room for the night. The ladies and I have traveled far. Please, might you have a room with a tub?"

"We can arrange for a tub to be brought to your room. And will you be needing one room or two?" the clerk inquired.

"Do you have a room with two beds?" She flashed him a smile.

"Yes, we do. That will be three dollars and the tub will be

an extra charge," said the clerk.

She raised her dark eyebrows at him.

The desk clerk ignored her. "That's a total of four dollars," he said.

She gathered coins from her drawstring purse and laid the money on the counter. She signed the registry book... *Miss Lily Baramore, The Cincinnati Theatrical Touring Company.*

"Well! Miss Baramore, do you perform on one of those floating theaters in Cincinnati?" asked the clerk. His attitude was much more cordial.

"The ladies and I have enjoyed working on the Floating Palace, not to mention a few other excursion steamers traveling the Ohio and Mississippi," answered Miss Baramore.

Samuel and S.W. were intently listening and found themselves captivated.

The desk clerk handed her the key. "I trust you will be satisfied with room four, at the end of the hall on the right. If there is anything more you need, please let me know."

"Thank you kindly," said Miss Baramore to the clerk.

"Follow me ladies and gentlemen." She waved her arm ushering them up the stairway. Samuel and S.W. looked at her in awe as they obediently carried the bags up the stairs to the end of the long hallway and waited on her to unlock the door. The charming young ladies entered the room and Samuel and

S.W. placed their bags just inside the door on the floor.

"You are so kind. Thank you so much for helping us," said Miss Baramore.

"It was our pleasure," said Samuel. He still had a sparkle in his eyes.

"It was nice meeting you ladies. Hope you have a pleasant stay while you're here," added S.W.

"Thank you," said Miss Baramore. Her companions were unpacking their bags as she continued to speak. "Oh, gentlemen... if you are going to be in town, perhaps you would be so kind as to join us later this afternoon?"

"Well... I... don't know..." Samuel was unusually hesitant.

"What Samuel means is that we will be leaving before noon, but we appreciate the invite," S.W. spoke for him.

"That's too bad. I thought you gentlemen might be interested in learning of a business where you could earn a little extra money," said Miss Baramore.

"What kind of business might that be?" S.W. inquired.

"If you could meet me in the hotel tavern at noon I could explain it in detail."

"Well, Miss Baramore, I reckon we could stay in town a little while longer," Samuel suddenly found his voice.

"Please, call me Lily. I will meet you in the tavern at noon."

As they descended the stairs Samuel said, "Ye know, I sure would like to get to know her better. She's right good lookin'.

The other ladies were pretty too."

"We better concentrate on getting some food and going home," S.W. sternly said as they entered the hotel tavern and proceeded to find a seat.

"No one is in here right now. We can get served and then head for home." S.W. was annoyed with Samuel.

"Ye mean we can't stay to get to know the ladies?" Samuel teased S.W.

"The ladies?" Mrs. Wilson inquired as she approached the table to serve them. "Why you interested?"

"It just strikes me a little odd, women travelin' alone. They might need someone to look after them." Samuel reasoned.

"Those women don't need looking after. They're probably chorus girls in one of those traveling variety shows. They might even work on one those riverboat saloons that the professional gamblers frequent. If it's a woman you're a looking for, look somewhere else," warned Mrs. Wilson.

"Why, Mrs. Wilson, it sounds like ye has visited some of those places." Samuel was curious and wanted to get a rise out of Mrs. Wilson. He and S.W. had become friends with Mrs. Wilson since they started coming to the tavern after making regular deliveries to the cabinetmaker.

"I have been to Cincinnati a few times. Some of the steamers are just like a palace, with grand staircases and carpeted floors; real nice furniture. You should be so lucky to see the gilded ceilings, and mirror-lined walls. They serve the finest food and drinks. The rich folks stay in the private cabins on the upper deck and the poor folks, well, they sleep on the freight decks."

"So, you been on a steamer, I mean a showboat?" asked S.W.

"I was part of the work crew. I washed dishes, shined glasses, polished the silver, and cleaned floors. I was just one of many servants," Mrs. Wilson fondly recalled. "Well, that's enough about me. You young fellas better heed my warning and stay away from those women. Now... what can I get for you?"

"We will take whatever you have ready," replied S.W. "Mrs. Wilson, I know the food here is good."

"We still have plenty of fried potatoes, ham and eggs. I'll fix you right up."

Just as she was placing their food on the table the older couple from the morning train and their little boy entered. They sat down at the long table with S.W. and Samuel. The little boy was restless, kicking his feet and fidgeting in his chair. "I'm thirsty, Mama," he cried out.

Mrs. Wilson came on the run with a pitcher of water, two mugs, and tin cup for the boy. "Now, now, little boy, I can take care of that." She poured water for all of them. "You folks ride on the train long?"

"Any train ride is too long for the boy and my wife, nevertheless, we survived it," reported the man. "We got on the train in Cin..."

Before he could finish speaking, two men stormed into the hotel tavern - their boots forcefully striking the hardwood floor with every step they took. They stood straight as arrows dressed in their black slouch hats, black scarves tied around their necks, and black buttoned down vests. They smelled of sweat and dirt from being on the riding trails too long. The hotel clerk looked stunned when they demanded the registry book. The handle of a Colt revolver protruded from under one of the men's vest.

"Look, we know you're hidin' those women!" One of the men yelled as he grabbed the thin clerk by the front of his shirt. "Now hand over that book!"

Nervously the clerk produced the book. They glanced at the book and became enraged. Both men turned toward the stairway. They rushed up the stairs, climbing the steps two at a time. They went directly to the end of the hall, room four, and shoved the door open, splintering the wood. Miss Baramore was sitting in a parlor chair. She had changed into a red silk robe.

The two men stood at the door. The enraged man yelled at Miss Baramore, "Where are they?" He pointed his finger at her. "You! You helped them cross the Ohio River and now you're hidin' them!" The man snarled like a mad dog when he spoke.

Miss Baramore remained calm sitting in the mahogany parlor chair. "Whatever are you talking about?"

The comment infuriated the man. He drew a knife from the leather made sheath which was attached to his belt and tied with a leather string around his leg.

"You're nothin' but a cheap riverboat whore pretending to be in the theater. Those women are the property of Mr. Sloan! Now you better start talkin' unless you want your pretty little face scarred up!"

Samuel and S.W. heard the violent commotion and rushed to help the women. Samuel crept in behind the man with the knife and grabbed his right wrist and placed his other arm around his neck forcing him to the floor. Once on the floor, Samuel was able to wrestle the man, causing him to release the knife. S.W. punched the other man in the jaw and kicked him in the stomach with such force that the man fell to the floor. Blood from the man's nose spewed and droplets of bright red blood appeared on the Persian carpet.

The violent man rapidly regained his strength and reached and grabbed for the knife on the floor. He was about to stab Samuel in the back when one of the men who had departed from the morning train, entered the room. Without warning the well-dressed man swiftly produced a knife of his own. The carved ivory knife handle shined as he hurled it at the man. The knife hit him in the wrist and went through his shirt sleeve, pinning his shirt to the floor. Mysteriously the same well-dressed man produced another knife and was about to take aim when suddenly a deep authoritative voice roared throughout the room.

"What's goin' on in here?" the sheriff demanded to know. He pointed his rifle at the men, while three of his men followed as backup with firearms drawn. Silence filled the room.

"You fellas got some explainin' to do. Throw down your weapons and empty your pockets! Men, tie their hands behind their backs!" The sheriff had a reputation for not backing down. He had been an experienced wagon master and scout, bringing settlers cross-country through the Appalachians to northwestern Ohio. He was a tall man with wide shoulders. His hair was graying, but his mustache was still very dark. There was an aura of mystery about him. It was in his eyes and on his face, amidst all those lines and furrows in his weathered dark skin. Maybe it was having lived with the Indians that made him so wise.

It wasn't long for the silence to be broken.

"Sheriff! I got an affidavit for the return of two fugitive slave women. Miss Baramore has helped them escape and is hidin' them!"

The sheriff reached down and removed the carved ivory handled knife from the bloody sleeve of the man's shirt which was pinned to the floor.

"Attractive knife," the sheriff said. He looked directly at the well-dressed man and stated, "You must be a gambler to afford a knife like this and them fancy clothes? I saw you get off the train. Where's your partner?"

The well-dressed man wearing his tailor-made suit coat remained silent.

Then the sheriff looked again at the man bleeding on the floor.

"Mr., you got blood all over your shirt and on this nice carpet." He waved his rifle in the air as he turned around.

"One of you men go get the doctor."

The sheriff ignored the man's statement concerning the affidavit and stepped near the chair where Miss Baramore was sitting.

"How are you Lily? Been a right long time since I seen you."

"Why, I'm just fine, now that your here." She smiled a polite smile.

"Sheriff!" yelled the bleeding man, "did you hear what I said?"

"Bounty Hunters..." For an instant, the sheriff's thoughts drifted to another time and place. Then, suddenly he yelled out, "I'm the sheriff here!"

"Those two women are the property of Mr. Sloan and I have the affidavit to prove it!" The bleeding man insisted on being heard.

"I don't see two women. The only woman I see is Lily," said the sheriff. "I don't care what affidavit you got. There are no women here. You and your partner can tell it to the judge!"

"When will that be?"

"Today or tomorrow. Today if we can locate him. Don't rightly know if he's in his office. He could be out of town. If that's the case, you can stay all night... in the jail," the sheriff laughed heartily.

"The doctor's here!" One of the men hollered.

"It's about time!" shouted the sheriff. "You men march these other fellas over to the jail and I'll be over shortly when the doctor is done here."

He rested his hand on Lily's shoulder and ordered Lily to stay put for a spell.

"The judge might want to ask you some questions."

"Me?" She held her hands over her heart. "Why I would never do anything to break the law. You know that, Sheriff."

"Yeah, Lily... I know," the sheriff spoke very softly with briefly noted affection.

"But, Sheriff..." Samuel started to protest when one of the sheriff's men nudged him on out the door.

"Hush up!" the man ordered. "You two young lads should have stayed out of this.

Samuel and S.W. sat in the jail the next morning waiting for the judge, but he never came. "How long are we gonna have to stay here?" Samuel was restless. He paced the floor of the small cell. It was hot and no air was moving.

"I wonder what became of those bounty hunters and those other two men who got off the morning train?" S.W. pondered the situation.

"What happened to those ladies? It's like they vanished," Samuel commented.

They could hear the front door open and the bell on the door clang. Samuel and S.W. starred at each other in silence, listening and hoping that the judge had arrived.

"Hello, sweetie. What did you bring me?" They could hear the sheriff's voice in the front office.

"Oh, silly, it's not for you. I came to see the fellas." It was Miss Baramore's voice they heard, talking to the Sheriff. She carried a large woven basket filled with food and drink. She put the basket down on the desk.

"Papa," she gently said, "you know the judge is out of town and won't be back until next week. He's visiting his family in Toledo. So, why don't you release those young fellas?"

He looked at her with his piercing dark brown eyes, then slowly walked back to the jail cell.

"You lads can go. Pick up your belongings in the front office. Lily will help you." The Sheriff walked to the front door and announced he was going over to the hotel tavern.

"I'll see you later, Papa."

The bell clanged again as he opened and shut the door.

Samuel and S.W. didn't waste any time getting to the front of the jail to collect their things.

"Why, hello fellas." The dimples in Miss Baramore's face were noticeably deep when she smiled. Samuel thought she looked like an angel.

"The Sheriff is your Pappy?" S.W. asked with a look of confusion on his face.

"The only Pappy I know." She lifted the basket from the desk and placed it over her arm. "I know you fellas want to get home, but I was hoping you would take some time to eat with me. While we are eating, I could explain everything. There is a beautiful shade tree right there to sit under." She pointed out the window to a huge oak tree.

Samuel quickly answered, "I reckon we could do that."

S.W. wasn't as anxious as Samuel to join Miss Baramore. "No thanks, Miss Baramore. Our folks will be wondering what happened to us. Our families will be worried sick."

"You need not worry. Papa sent word to your family that you are safe and you would be a day or two getting back. Come along, let's sit under the tree. I brought a blanket and food to eat and something to drink."

She opened the door and proceeded outside with the basket over her arm. Samuel and S.W. followed. They sat comfortably on a blanket under the large shade tree eating and drinking and enjoying the company of Miss Baramore, whom they were now calling Lily.

"Thank you for coming to my rescue," she said as she handed Samuel a half pint flask of apple brandy that she brought from the tavern. "My Papa... I mean the Sheriff, has told me all about you. You are honest and hard workingmen. Just as I expected you to be when first we met."

She also handed S.W. a half pint flask of apple brandy. Lily gently lifted a pie from the basket. "Mrs. Wilson made this delicious blackberry pie," Lily smiled as she served the pie. Lily's dark brown eyes and dimples in her face were immediately noticeable in the bright sunlight. Samuel briefly entertained thoughts of a romantic interlude even though he knew it would never happen.

S.W. didn't see her in the same light as Samuel although he did consider her to be most attractive. He sensed that his good friend was having all the wrong ideas about Miss Lily. Although S.W. wanted to make a hasty departure, he took a bite of the pie.

"I hope you can explain all this in a very short time," S.W. snapped at her.

"I truly want to explain." She took a drink of her own apple brandy and then continued. "I had held onto the hope that you would be of some assistance in helping us to travel further north. I sense that you can be trusted. You see... I assist runaway slaves into Canada."

S.W. found the conversation more interesting as he considered what she was telling them.

"The women you met on the train are mulatto. You really didn't take notice of their color and neither did anyone else. My experience of working in the theater contributed to their disguise and their fashionable attire." She paused to see how they were going to react. When neither of them made a comment, she continued, "They are Sloan's property." Lily hesitated for a moment.

She looked at them and again waited for a response. All the while, they were conjuring thoughts in their heads about what a southern plantation must be like. Samuel was sitting on the ground leaning against the tree. He focused on the brandy. S.W. was eating a bite of pie. Neither of them had ever been any further south than to cross the Ohio River into Covington, Kentucky, to the tobacco fields. Newspaper articles, pictures, and stories from Mr. McClure at the general store were as close to the real South as they had ever been. A slave plantation was unimaginable.

"Finish the story," Samuel suddenly insisted.

"My mother worked in the theater on the Floating Palace. Sloan was frequenting the riverboat saloons, variety shows, and theaters when they met. Shortly after my mother met Sloan, she left the Palace and went to work in a traveling variety show to get away from him. That's when she met Papa."

"Papa was a scout on the wagon train moving cross-country when he met my mother. He loved my mother even though she carried another man's child. He married her and raised me as his own."

"Those two men who got off the train, were they with you?" S.W. asked.

"They were." Lily reached into the basket for a plate of cheese and a loaf of bread. "They left on the morning train."

"Where are the ladies?" S.W. looked puzzled.

She passed the cheese and bread to Samuel. "They have safe passage north."

"And where are those knife wielding bounty hunters?" asked S.W. as he tore off a piece of bread to eat with the cheese.

"They are far from here." She nibbled on bread and cheese. "Papa has made sure of that."

"Ye got involved in the underground and ye carry a vengeance for Sloan. Tis a mighty dangerous undertaking for a woman." Samuel was looking at her differently now. She was not only beautiful, but a woman with a purpose. He liked that.

"That is why men, such as you, must get involved. We need your help. By helping the slaves, we can weaken the south. We must smuggle more runaways. A little while longer and it will be too dangerous."

Lily had captured their interest. She knew they were honest men and that she may need their help sometime in the future. She continued telling them how she met Sloan.

"I met Sloan on one of the steamers. A fine steamer it was. He went down to the freight deck to attend to his "property." I waited until I was sure he was gone. I knew he would be gambling for hours. That's how I was able to locate the women and help them escape. Of course, I had help."

"That was mighty risky," said Samuel. "This fella, Sloan, do ye know where he is?"

"His plantation is in Louisiana. He frequently travels the Mississippi and the Ohio rivers. He is a shrewd and cunning man."

"This man ye speak of be ye father," said Samuel.

"The only father I have is the Sheriff. I will never lay claim to such a man as Sloan."

Samuel got up and leaned against the tree. Lily held out her hand for him to help her up. Samuel took hold of her hand and when she stood up he could smell the scent of rose oil in her hair. He quickly held her by her shoulders to steady her then he backed away.

"Oh, please excuse me," she said as she got a steady footing.

"We need to get going!" S.W. glared at Samuel to get him moving.

"Will I see you again?" Lily asked. "And will you at least consider my request?"

"Well, I don't rightly know about that. We're not looking for trouble." S.W. got up and put on his straw hat.

"Thanks for the hospitality, Miss Lily," responded Samuel. He smiled a respectful smile and tipped his hat to her. He knew S.W. was right. It sounded like a pretty risky endeavor, on the other hand, meeting Miss Lily had changed his way of thinking. There was a lot to consider. The country was changing.

S.W. and Samuel abruptly left Lily standing under the tree with her basket of food and apple brandy. They never looked back. They took long strides down the dirt street right past the hotel, tavern, and train station. The Sheriff caught up with them as they were walking to the livery stable.

"You lads leaving town?" questioned the Sheriff.

"We sure are!" answered S.W.

"Well, be sure to tell your Aunt Sarah the sheriff said hello."

"You acquainted with Aunt Sarah?"

"Sure am, we go back a long way," he said. "You be sure to tell her I said hello. Well, I hope you lads come back real soon. We always got a bed for you at the jail." He chuckled and tipped his hat as he proceeded to walk across the street.

S.W. would like to have inquired more about Aunt Sarah, but it was the wrong time for such questions when all he really wanted to do was to get out of town.

Chapter Four
A Stranger in the House

Samuel was quiet on the ride home. He and S.W. were weary from lack of sleep due to spending the previous night in jail. The constant turning of the wagon wheels on the rough road formed a trail of dust behind the wagon. The wagon was empty and the horses were able to travel much faster now. It was just past noon by the time they reached Perry Township and they could see the road sign pointing to the little village of Franconia. The horses sensed familiar surroundings and Samuel held tight to the reins to keep them at bay as they got near the home place.

When they got closer to the house they could see Charlotte and another woman hanging clothes on the line. Gilbert was drawing water from the well and was pouring the water into a huge copper kettle which hung over an open fire.

Samuel drew back on the reins. "*Whoa*, horse. *Whoa!*" he called out and brought the wagon to a halt. S.W. jumped down from the wagon. Charlotte turned just in time to see Samuel waving at them as he drove away. Charlotte waved back. S.W. immediately headed to the well as he had become extremely thirsty on the ride home. He removed his straw hat, got a cold drink from the well and splashed cold water on his face.

Charlotte called out to him, "S.W. we weren't expecting you home today! The sheriff sent word to Aunt Sarah that you might be home in a couple of days! Are you alright? Do you want something to eat?"

"I'm fine!" S.W. walked to the back porch and took a towel from a wooden peg on the porch wall. He dried his face and hands before sitting down on the steps to rest.

Charlotte rushed over to sit beside him on the steps. She put her arms around him. "I'm so glad you're home!"

"It's good to be home! I wouldn't want to spend another night in that place," S.W. proclaimed.

"You mean the jail? What happened?" Gilbert begged as he too took a seat on the steps near S.W.

"Yes, the calaboose!" S.W. spoke sharply at Gilbert.

"The calaboose?" Gilbert looked puzzled.

"The jail! Gilbert, I'll tell you about it later!"

"You promise?" Gilbert asked.

"I promise, little brother. It can be your bedtime story." S.W. was grumpy with Gilbert.

"You always treat me like a baby," Gilbert whined.

S.W. quickly changed the subject. "I see you got a helper!"

"Yeah, Aunt Sarah brought Cora out to help around here!" Gilbert announced loudly. "She's real nice and a real good cook too!"

Cora finished hanging the blanket on the clothesline then walked toward the porch where they were all sitting.

Charlotte looked up at Cora and said, "I'm sorry, I didn't introduce you. This is my brother... S.W.!"

Gilbert hastily added to the introduction, "S.W. is short for Sylvester Wilson. He hates his name. We call him S.W. and sometimes he calls himself Wilson."

Cora dried her hands on her apron and reached out to shake S.W.'s hand.

"It's nice to meet you. I've heard lots about you." She spoke very softly. Cora smiled at him and then asked, "What would you like me to call you?"

He firmly held her hand. "Good to meet you too. You can call me S.W. just like everyone else does. Will you be staying long?" He stared with a wide-eyed gaze into her mystifying green eyes. Then without warning he felt as though he were under a spell. He just sat there on the steps feeling very weak. He took a detailed survey of the tall, thin, young woman with the copper red hair and fair freckled skin. The sleeves of her white cotton blouse were rolled up above her elbows. The front of her blouse and apron were wet from wringing out the laundry.

She startled him when she spoke to answer his question about how long she would be staying.

"I'm here for the rest of the summer and harvest time too. At least that's what Miss Sarah tells me. Do you have any objections?" Cora's voice was soft and hypnotic.

S.W. didn't respond at first, then he slowly answered and let go of her hand. "Why, no, I suppose not." The truth was he did mind having a stranger in the house. Cora's presence had taken him completely by surprise and it took him awhile to regain his composure. He suddenly realized he must keep his wits about him. He immediately asked for the whereabouts of Amy Ann.

"She went with Aunt Sarah for a few days. She's a comin' back on Sunday," Gilbert replied.

Gilbert got up to wrap another rope around a tree so they could hang more quilts and blankets to dry. Then S.W. went over to help secure the rope around the tree limb. Charlotte and Cora continued doing the washing.

"Where's big brother, Oliver?" S.W. sounded intent on getting an answer.

"He's over at the Donaldsons' helpin' get the hay in. They got a new horse-drawn wooden rake!" Gilbert said with excitement in his voice.

"Why ain't you over there?" S.W. asked in a stern voice.

Now, S.W. felt like he was back in control of himself.

"Well, who's gonna' pack the water for the washin'?" Gilbert defended himself.

"Getting the hay in is pretty important!" S.W. put on his straw hat and headed to the barn. Gilbert followed him to the barn to get a scythe and a rake.

"The Donaldsons' got plenty a help! Do we gotta' go? Anyhow you just got home. Ain't you tired?" Gilbert complained as he trudged up the path to the barn. All of Gilbert's efforts to persuade S.W. to stay home failed.

"Neighbors help one another. It's the right thing to do!" S.W. was determined to get over to the Donaldsons' place. S.W. walked faster and Gilbert had a hard time keeping up with him.

When they came back from the barn, Charlotte called out to them, "We will be over as soon as we can! I know Mrs. Donaldson will need help with the children at supper time!"

S.W. and Gilbert walked side-by-side down the dirt road. S.W. carried the heavy long handled scythe over his shoulder and Gilbert carried the rake. As they got close to the farm, they could see the men working in the hayfield. It was late in the afternoon when they arrived and the men were raking the hay by hand into long wind-rows. S.W. and Gilbert walked through the tall fresh grass to join them, the smell of fresh cut hay still lingering in the air.

"Looks like you might get done early today," S.W spoke to Jake Donaldson.

Jake and S.W. were working side-by-side in the row. Gilbert moved up a row to rake with two other men and Oliver was working in the row across the field.

"Some of the men stayed to help do the turning and shaking-out the hay to dry. Pa's using the new hay rake so, we should get done early." Jake rested on the long-handled rake for a minute or two.

"Most likely Samuel doesn't know you're haymaking or he would be here," said S.W. "It was afternoon when Samuel and I got back from Ottawa."

"I heard you fellas were delayed for a spell. Word was you spent the night in jail," Jake gave out a hearty laugh.

"Word sure travels fast around here," S.W. replied as he continued working.

The afternoon went by fast and soon they heard the farm bell ringing out a clear signal for the men to come eat. The men slowly walked to the farmhouse to clean up and get ready or supper.

Mrs. Donaldson had a tubful of warm water and a bar of soap ready for them on the back porch. Long tables were made from wooden sawhorses with wooden planks laid on top. There was plenty of food and drinks for everyone. The men helped themselves to the delicious food and sat on the ground under the shade trees in the yard.

Charlotte and Cora were on the porch helping Mrs. Donaldson with the younger children. The Donaldsons' had a large family and people were always coming and going. Oliver, Jake, S.W., and Gilbert relaxed on the ground under one of the huge trees in the yard. They sat in the grass dipping bread into their bowls of vegetable soup. Gilbert held out his tin drinking cup when one of the Donaldson girls came around with a pitcher of sassafras tea.

"You better get some of Mama's blackberry pie," the young girl said as she walked through the grass with bare feet. It was common for the Donaldson children to go barefoot in the summertime.

Jake Donaldson proceeded to inquire about S.W.'s trip. Oliver and Gilbert were eager to hear about it, too. S.W. seemed reluctant to talk about it, nonetheless they relentlessly teased him about his night in jail. So, S.W. recounted the event.

"We left in the early morning when it was still cool and we got there plenty early. We delivered the lumber to the cabinetmaker and then took the horses to the livery stable. By then we were really hungry, so we headed on over to the hotel tavern. The morning train had just arrived and the passengers were departing just as we got there." S.W. dipped bread to sop up the last bit of broth in the bottom of his bowl.

"Well... go on... tell us more," begged Gilbert.

"Three very nice looking young women departed the train and were standing on the station platform waiting for the porter to deliver their bags to the hotel. Samuel dallied around by the entrance door so he could help them. We carried their bags to the front desk and then on up to their room."

S.W. drank the last drop of sassafras tea from the tin cup and got up to get more.

"Don't go away now! This is just getting interesting!" exclaimed Oliver.

"Well," said S.W. as he removed his straw hat to scratch his head, "I think Samuel was a might smitten with Lily... I mean Miss Baramore."

"Who's Lily?" Gilbert's voice sounded urgent. His young mind was filled with intensity.

"Lily got off the train with the other two women. She registered at the desk as Lily Baramore from The Cincinnati Theatrical Touring Company."

S.W. walked away with the tin cup in his hand and returned with a full cup of tea and a big piece of blackberry pie. He sat down in the grass in the shade.

"Tell us more!" Gilbert was becoming more impatient by the second.

"Then two trail riders busted in and took the desk clerk by surprise. They demanded to know where the women were."

S.W. took another bite of the blackberry pie and then added, "One of the men roughed up the desk clerk and grabbed the registry book away from him. Then they rushed up the stairs looking for the women, only to find the women had vanished."

Then Gilbert asked S.W., "What do you mean the women vanished?"

"The two trail riders turned out to be bounty hunters. I reckon someone got word to the women that they were being followed and they got out the backway. The two women seem to have vanished, except for Lily. Lily was still in the room when the men busted open the door."

S.W. gathered up his dirty bowl and spoon to take to the house. He stood for a while with the dirty dishes in his hands and continued to explain how he and Samuel were thrown in jail.

"Samuel and I heard a ruckus upstairs and we ran up the stairs. One of the men was threatening Lily with a knife. Samuel was quick to attack him and I fought off the other man."

S.W. took a drink of tea from the tin cup. "It was just then, that another fella entered the room. I'm pretty sure he was a riverboat gambler. He sure was quick with a knife. This other fella... the bounty hunter, was about to stab Samuel in the back when the gambler threw his knife and hit the bounty hunter in the wrist. That knocked the knife out of his hand and pinned the sleeve of his shirt to the floor. That's when the Sheriff and his deputies burst into the room!"

"Why were they after the women?" Jake questioned.

"The women turned out to be slaves. The bounty hunter kept yelling about a man named Sloan. Said he had papers to prove that they were his slaves."

"You mean you couldn't tell they were slaves?" Jake's interest had turned to curiosity.

"No... we had no idea! We learned later that they were mulatto. Because Lily was from the theater and all, she was able to disguise them." Then S.W. turned to walk toward the house, but he quickly turned back around to tell them, "Oh, and the sheriff... he turned out to be Lily's Pappy." He didn't tell them that the sheriff and Aunt Sarah were old friends. He needed to learn more about that.

Gilbert instantly remarked, "Well, ain't that somethin! This woman, Lily... her Pappy is the sheriff! She must've fooled everyone!"

"She belongs to that antislavery movement... the underground railroad." Jake perceived. "She must be pretty clever."

"I hear that's pretty dangerous," said Oliver. "We want to know more about that woman... Lily," demanded Oliver.

S.W. turned around to face Oliver and said, "You need to ask Samuel about her."

S.W. said goodnight to everyone and continued to the

house with the dirty dishes in his hands. He figured he gave them enough to think on and talk about. He knew the folks would be hashing over the account for days, maybe even weeks. It tickled him to give them a temporary distraction in their ordinary lives.

As S.W. walked through the yard to the house he overheard some of the men talking about the Wide Awakes and Lincoln's Presidential Campaign.

"Well, just let me tell ya... those Wide Awakes are all young men from the north. Them young fellas all wear uniforms made of shiny black cloth. Midnight... that's when they rally. Each one has a lit torch and they fall into marching companies." Old Dan Sellers was having a good old time informing the others of the parade he had seen in Fort Wayne, Indiana.

Another man asked, "Who are these Wide Awakes? And how do you know 'bout 'em?"

"I said... I seen them parading around in Fort Wayne one night!" repeated Old Dan. "Other folks say they've seen them in Toledo and Columbus. I've absolutely seen them for myself!"

S.W. kept on walking, carrying his dirty dishes. He was too tired to join in the discussion, but he too wondered, "Who are these Wide Awakes?" He thought he might read about them in the paper at Mr. McClure's General Store. Mr. McClure knew everything that was going on.

When S.W. got to the front porch, Cora was sitting in the porch swing holding the Donaldsons' youngest child.

"Hello, S.W.," she softly spoke so as not to disturb the sleeping child. "You can take those dirty dishes around back. That's where Mrs. Donaldson and the older girls are washing up the dishes."

"I'll do just that... take the dirty dishes around back," said S.W. while he leaned against the porch banister for a moment to rest.

S.W. silently thought to himself, "It's odd that the Donaldson family have welcomed and accepted Cora when she is just a stranger. She is friendly enough and even helpful. She doesn't act like a stranger around folks and she seems to fit right in. Still there's just something amiss about her."

Cora noticed S.W. had suddenly become quiet and was looking rather weary. Cora questioned him, "The wagon is around back. Are you fellas ready to go?"

"I am. It's been a long day. I can't speak for Gilbert and Oliver though. They like to talk when they get the chance. I'll just go around back and rest in the wagon while you and Charlotte get ready."

When S.W. got to the back-porch Charlotte collected the dirty dishes and put them in a pan of hot soapy water.

"Thanks for all the good food, Mrs. Donaldson," S.W. said.

"Thanks be to you for helping out today. You look mighty tired. Are you going home now?" she asked.

"Yes, and if you won't be needing Cora and Charlotte, they better be going home, too," S.W. said.

"Why, that's fine. You folks have always been good about helping. Oh, say... that Cora is a good worker. She digs right in to help a body. She sure has been a big help with the children tonight," Mrs. Donaldson commented.

S.W. didn't respond to Mrs. Donaldsons' comment regarding Cora. He simply departed saying, "Goodnight, Mrs. Donaldson."

It wasn't long before Gilbert ran around to the back of the house where he found S.W. resting in the back of the wagon.

"I guess I'm just in time to ride home." Gilbert climbed in the back of the wagon with S.W.

"I heard Old Dan Sellers talkin' 'bout the Wide Awakes. Who are they?" Gilbert urgently wanted an answer.

"Don't know and don't care," S.W. answered.

"Well, I can ask Old Dan, the next time I see him." Gilbert was determined to find out.

"What's a keepin' Charlotte and Cora?" Gilbert asked.

The words were just out of his mouth when he saw them coming around the corner of the house.

"We were just saying goodnight to everyone," said Charlotte. "Oliver said he would walk home later. He sure loves talking to the men folk. It's hard to drag him home when he comes here."

Cora climbed up onto the wagon seat beside Charlotte.

"The Donaldsons surely seem like nice folks," said Cora. "I just love their children."

"Yes, they are good folks. There's never a dull moment at their place with so many children running around," Charlotte said as she got situated on the wagon seat. Charlotte took the reins in hand and gently tapped the horse on the hind quarters, making a clicking sound with her tongue against the roof of her mouth to get the horse moving.

It was a quiet trip going home with a picturesque evening sky of vivid pink and red colors streaming across the horizon, creating the end to a busy day.

Chapter Five
Illusive Hearts

Morning came all too soon. S.W. was still sleeping when he heard the door on the woodstove clang shut. He jumped up from his bed and put on clean trousers, fastened his suspenders over a clean white cotton shirt and put on clean socks. Then he pulled on his boots and walked into the kitchen where Cora was washing dishes.

"Good morning sleepyhead," Cora teasingly said as her green eyes drew him closer.

For a brief moment, he thought about what it would be like to hold her close in his arms, to tenderly kiss her on the lips and stroke her beautiful hair. She must have sensed his very thoughts as she quickly busied herself with kitchen tasks.

Her long copper colored hair was pulled back with a ribbon and flowed down her back as she hadn't yet braided her hair for the day. She was undeniably beautiful and glowing this morning. The green cotton dress she wore made her green eyes more noticeable. It seemed to S.W. that she looked very beautiful standing there in the kitchen as the morning sunlight came through the window. She reminded him of a picture of a woman he had once seen in a big city newspaper advertisement for powder and perfume. He quickly turned his head to avoid her seeing him stare. He wondered why someone with her good looks didn't have a beau, a suitor or even yet... a husband?

Quickly he stated, "I sure didn't aim to sleep so late. Where is everyone?"

"Oliver went to McClure's General Store to pick up a few things and Gilbert went along. Charlotte went along too. She wants to stop at the Truby home to visit with the girls for a spell. That just leaves you and me." Cora smiled a broad smile and continued cleaning off the table.

S.W. poured warm water in the wash pan and washed his face. Cora poured hot coffee in a cup with a saucer and then offered to fix him something to eat.

"This coffee is plenty, thanks anyway," he said. "I need to go check the fence line."

Not only did S.W. find something amiss about Cora, but he was finding it hard to fight off his attraction to her. He never thought he would be attracted to anyone but Adaline and he felt guilty for entertaining such thoughts. He packed his coffee cup and saucer to the back porch to drink and then went to check the fence.

S.W. was almost done walking the fence line when he saw the wagon coming in the distance, so he started walking back to the house to meet them. When he got to the house, Gilbert was sitting on the porch steps eating broken pieces of stick candy from a small tin container that he had bought from McClure's General store. S.W. studied the small tin box of candy as the scent of sassafras, horehound, cinnamon, and cloves emanated from the box.

"Have a bite," Gilbert said as he offered the small tin box of candy to S.W.

"Thanks." S.W. lifted a small piece of cinnamon candy from the tin. "Where did you get money to buy candy?"

"I been doin' some chores for Mr. McClure and Old Dan Sellers. Mr. McClure still ain't feelin' so good from that bump he took on his head, so he lets me help out at the store."

"That's mighty secretive of you. How come you never mentioned it?"

"I'm allowed to have secrets! Why don't you mind your own business?"

"You are my business, little brother," said S.W. He was grinning at Gilbert.

Gilbert put the lid back on the small tin box and put it in his pants pocket. When he stood up, a paper fell on the ground. S.W. quickly picked it up.

"What's this?" S.W. asked. He unfolded the publication and began to read it. It was a Wide Awakes promotional letter and meeting announcement from the Toledo Newspaper...

Lincoln Wide Awakes

The members of this organization are notified to present themselves at their hall punctually at 8 o'clock, as business of importance to all will be transacted. All Republican young men wishing to unite with the Club will please attend on Saturday night, Aug. 25th.

"Just where did you get this friendly publication?" asked S.W. after he finished reading it aloud.

"Some passerby left it at the store when he came through," Gilbert reported. He reached for the publication, but S.W. held onto it.

"Gilbert, you ain't old enough to join up with The Wide Awakes. I think I best hold onto this for safe keeping."

Surprisingly, Gilbert didn't argue with him. Gilbert simply sat back down to discuss what the passerby had to say.

"Those Wide Awakes are all young fellas. They wear uniforms and march in parades! They give speeches and campaign for Lincoln. They meet up... in Philadelphia and New York... they're everywhere! And... I even heard the folks down south are real scared of 'em!"

Gilbert was thrilled to have met the passerby and he was eager to attend one of the rallies. He was silent for a minute. He expected S.W. to reprimand him.

"Mr. McClure has the latest newspaper from Toledo with pictures of the Wide Awakes! There's a meetin' in Toledo too!" Gilbert continued speaking with much enthusiasm. "I want that publication back! It's gonna' stay put right here in my pocket!"

Reluctantly, S.W. handed the article back to Gilbert. Gilbert folded the paper and put it back in his pocket.

Before Gilbert had the chance to walk away, Oliver, Charlotte, and Cora came out onto the back porch of the old log house to sit. Cora nodded her head and politely smiled at S.W. as she sat down on the bench next to him. Her long hair was tightly pulled back into a braided bun. This was a new hairstyle that S.W. hadn't seen before and once again he found himself momentarily staring at Cora.

Charlotte immediately noticed S.W.'s interest in Cora's hair and she wondered if he was secretly having thoughts about her.

"Oh, Cora, you are so clever with braiding hair. Do you think you could braid my hair to look just like yours?" Charlotte implored.

"Of course, I'd be happy to," Cora smiled.

Charlotte was still wearing the black cotton dress with

white-laced collar and lace edging on the sleeves along with matching bonnet. She had worn it to the Trubys'.

"Why you wearin' your good clothes?" Gilbert asked Charlotte.

"I wore it over to Adaline's and Betsy's so they could see it. Cora let me wear it. It doesn't fit her anymore and it just fits me. And I'm going to wear it to church tomorrow."

Charlotte was looking very proud with her petticoat making her dress look very full and when she whirled around the ruffles and lace narrowly showed beneath her dress.

"Church! Tomorrow?" Gilbert complained. "It's Sunday again?

"We always go to church on Sunday and you know it." Charlotte was gruff with him.

"Aunt Sarah is comin' tomorrow. She's bringin' Amy Ann back home. Remember?" Gilbert reminded her.

"She won't be here until late in the day. We have plenty of time to go to church," said Charlotte.

Cora hastily offered to stay home to prepare a nice meal and have everything looking good for Aunt Sarah's visit.

"And I will stay home and help Cora," Gilbert clearly rushed to make the statement.

"There, that's all settled! Now we can get to work," Oliver said. "I need your help little brother!" Oliver seemed to be annoyed with their conversation.

"Where we goin'?" asked Gilbert.

"We are going to the Donaldsons' to finish getting in the hay," said Oliver. "Are you coming along S.W.?"

"I reckon so." S.W. got up to join them.

Gilbert saw Cora smiling at S.W. and he thought it was amusing. S.W. saw Gilbert grinning and gave Gilbert a little brotherly shove as they headed out.

"That Cora is right good lookin'," said Gilbert as he climbed into the wagon.

"I never noticed," S.W. replied in an attempt to put an end to Gilbert's comments.

Gilbert continued to tease S.W. about Cora until he spotted Samuel walking down the road.

"Look there's Samuel! He must be goin' to help make hay too!" Gilbert shouted. Gilbert's curiosity had been building and now he had the opportunity to question Samuel about Lily.

Oliver stopped the wagon and Samuel climbed in the back to ride along. As soon as Samuel climbed in, Gilbert began to coax and plead with Samuel to tell him all about Lily. Finally, Samuel was persuaded and he seemed to thoroughly enjoy giving his account.

Samuel was still talking about Lily when they reached the Donaldsons' property. Gilbert and Oliver were intrigued. They listened with great interest and had lots of questions.

Oliver wanted to know more about the sheriff. "So, the Sheriff is Lily's Pappy. Ain't that interesting?"

"Yeah, and how does the Sheriff know Aunt Sarah?" Gilbert asked as he jumped down from the wagon.

"Well, Gilbert, 'tis a mystery," Samuel said as he was walking away carrying a rake over his shoulder.

"Let's get started!" Oliver commanded and walked on ahead of them. "Looks like plenty of help in the hayfields today, maybe we can get home early."

Oliver was not so impressed with the story of the alluring Miss Lily as he had just recently found a new interest of his own, although he hadn't told anyone about her just yet. She lived in the next county and he knew that a long distance courtship was going to be difficult, still, he was determined to see her again.

Oliver's observation about finishing work early was correct and they headed for home long before dark. Oliver was unusually quiet on the ride home until Gilbert enticed him into talking about his whereabouts the previous Saturday night.

"Oliver, you sure got home late last Saturday night. You must a found yourself a gal at that church meetin' you say you went to." Gilbert questioned his big brother.

"That's for me to know," answered Oliver.

"So, you don't deny it. There is a gal," said Gilbert.

"I don't deny it. There is a gal and that's the end of it," Oliver firmly stated.

Gilbert knew from the tone of Oliver's voice not to ask any more questions; however, he was prepared to find out more even if it took a little more time to investigate.

S.W. and Samuel were surprised to learn of Oliver's courtship. They didn't ask any questions as they knew Oliver was a very private person.

Once back home and inside the house Gilbert couldn't wait to tell Charlotte, Amy Ann, and Cora about Oliver's new interest. Oliver just grinned at the girls and went about his business as they tried to gain information. The evening was spent in joyful conversation and hoping for bright futures. S.W. got out his mouth harp and Gilbert located the fiddle. Amy Ann and Charlotte danced together and Cora took the opportunity to just sit down and enjoy the music.

Chapter Six
August 19, 1860
What's Wrong with Cora?

It was Sunday morning and everyone had gone to church except for Cora and Gilbert. Cora sat at the kitchen table with her head down in prayer. What would she do when harvest time was over? She had no family, no one to turn to. She considered moving to Toledo, Ohio, where she might easily find work. Cora didn't know anyone there and she quickly dismissed the thought.

"Maybe Toledo? No," she said out loud. "I really like it here and I'd like to stay."

"Then stay," said Gilbert.

"How long have you been standing there?" asked Cora. She was glad she hadn't said anything else for Gilbert to hear.

"Just long enough to hear you say that you really like it here and you want to stay."

"I was just thinking, that's all." Cora got up from the table and went to sit in the rocking chair on the back porch.

Gilbert followed her and sat on the porch railing. He whittled on a small piece of wood with his favorite pocket knife.

"You got folks 'round here?" asked Gilbert.

"No, my folks are all gone. I'm on my own," said Cora as she rocked in the chair.

"I know how you feel," he said soulfully.

Cora continued to explain. "I been on my own since I was fourteen. I lived with my grandmother for about a year then she took sick and died. I've been working as a servant for folks ever since."

"Well, you can just stay here. Aunt Sarah will be just fine with that." Gilbert made the statement sound official.

Cora laughed at Gilbert and said, "She has already been too good to me. I appreciate all she has done."

"How did you get to know Aunt Sarah?" Gilbert inquired.

"I was working in Cincinnati for an old friend of Miss Sarah's. Mrs. Johnson was her name. My job was to care for Mrs. Johnson as she was getting along in years and she needed a companion. I wasn't just a companion, I cleaned house and cooked and cared for her every need. It was common for Miss Sarah to come visit Mrs. Johnson. Whenever Miss Sarah came to visit she would stay for a few days. I got to know Miss Sarah pretty well."

"Sounds like a pretty good job. How long did you stay?" Gilbert was taking the story all in as he whittled on the stick of wood.

"I worked in the big house for seven years. Then one day Mrs. Johnson received a letter from her nephew who lived in Pittsburgh. Mrs. Johnson read the letter and became very upset. Her nephew was coming to visit. I remember Mrs. Johnson saying... he was nothing but a scoundrel."

"Well, what happened? You mean he came to visit for a spell?" Gilbert asked as he continued to focus on whittling the small piece of wood.

"What I mean is, he became a permanent houseguest and he had no intentions of leaving." Cora rocked in the chair.

"Gee, why didn't the old lady make him leave?" Gilbert asked.

Cora continued to explain the situation. "Well, when her nephew first arrived he was well-dressed and charming. He looked like a well-to-do businessman, but as time went on he became very aggressive with Mrs. Johnson. He was always able to persuade her to give him money for his reckless business adventures and all this made old Mrs. Johnson very upset and ill."

"I bet Aunt Sarah would have kicked him out on his rear. Why didn't you tell her 'bout it?" Gilbert was tensing up.

"Well, Gilbert, I did notify Miss Sarah, but I didn't see the dark side of him until it was too late. Miss Sarah was on her way to Cincinnati when Mrs. Johnson suddenly became very sick. Her doctor said she had pneumonia and there was nothing that could be done to save her." Cora paused for a moment in deep thought and then said, "The very thought of him makes me cringe."

Gilbert took some time to consider the situation before speaking, "That's too bad the old lady got upset and got sick... and died! Does her nephew still live there?"

"He took over everything after Mrs. Johnson's death. So, you see... I had nowhere to live and very little money when this all happened. Thanks be to Miss Sarah for agreeing to let me live in and work for her."

"Ahhh, gee, it's too bad the old lady didn't leave you a little somethin'." Gilbert folded his pocket knife and put it away. "I sure do wish you could stay here," said Gilbert as he handed Cora the small hand carved figure of a dog.

Cora marveled at the small hand carved creation and lovingly smiled at Gilbert as she held it tightly in the palm of her hand.

"You see, Gilbert, I was just thinking about returning to Miss Sarah's place. I really owe her a lot. Gilbert, you are too kind! Now I really must get everything done before the folks get back from church." Cora stood up to stretch after sitting for so long.

"Gilbert, would you dig up some new potatoes and carrots from the garden?"

Gilbert was unusually compliant. He jumped up and grabbed a bucket and a potato fork from the back porch and went directly to the garden.

Cooking for so many was quite challenging, yet it was just a short time before Cora had dinner cooking on the wood burning stove. Just when she thought she had everything in order the dogs started barking. Cora and Gilbert looked out the front door and they could see a buggy coming toward the house.

"Well, for goodness sake, is it that time already?" Now Cora was getting nervous about preparing the meal on time.

"I reckon that's the Truby's following in behind," said Gilbert.

"Do you think they will stop by too?" asked Cora.

"If they do, they won't stay. Mrs. Truby will want to get home, straight away," answered Gilbert. "That's how she is," he added.

Oliver tied the horse and buggy to the post in front of the house and S.W. helped Charlotte down out of the buggy. Samuel came in behind them with their two-seater horse-drawn buggy. Betsy and Adaline were riding in the back seat of the buggy. Mrs. Truby sat in the front with Samuel. S.W. hurried over to greet Mrs. Truby and he offered his hand to help her down.

"No, no, only Betsy and Adaline stay to help. I must go home," Mrs. Truby said in her broken English. "Is alright for girls to stay?"

"Sure! Cora and Charlotte will be glad for the help," S.W. answered. The surprise visit had caught him off guard. They never mentioned stopping by when they were at church. He quickly ran to help Betsy and Adaline down from the buggy.

"Ye be bringin' the women folk home later?" asked Samuel.

"Surely will!" replied S.W.

"Tis good then," said Samuel. Mrs. Truby smiled and waved goodbye.

"Betsy and Adaline have come to help us," Charlotte reported to Cora as they entered the house.

"It's always nice to have help in the kitchen," Cora responded with a welcoming smile. Now Cora was flustered because she wasn't expecting so much company for dinner. She certainly wasn't expecting Adaline and her sister, Betsy.

Charlotte handed Betsy and Adaline aprons to protect their clothing while they helped in the kitchen and she placed an apron over her own good clothes.

Gilbert stood staring at the young women when they entered the kitchen. They were looking very attractive dressed in their Sunday clothes. They wore plain black dresses with white tatted lace around the collar and sleeves.

"Gilbert, it's not nice to stare. You get out of the kitchen so we can get to work," ordered Charlotte.

"I'll be more than glad to go!" Gilbert stomped out the backdoor.

Gilbert had just walked out onto the porch when he saw Aunt Sarah's buggy coming. He peeked back inside to alert them that more company was coming.

"It's Aunt Sarah!" Gilbert shouted.

Gilbert stood at the hitching post waiting for them.

"Hello, my darling Gilbert," said Aunt Sarah. Gilbert opened the buggy door and helped her and Amy Ann down.

"Hello to you, Aunt Sarah."

Henry was looking very stylish in his Sunday clothes. A white cotton shirt with a vest, a black coat and shiny black polished boots.

"Henry, you're lookin' dapper today," Gilbert said.

"Thank you, Mr. Gilbert." Henry continued with the horse and buggy to a place in the shade.

Amy Ann walked toward the house carrying her parasol and a small draw-string purse. Charlotte was standing on the porch waiting to greet them.

"Why, Amy Ann, you look so..." Charlotte was lost for words.

"Grown up?" asked Amy Ann.

"Why, yes... grown up, exactly what I was thinking. Grown up, wearing that beautiful dress. Just look at the lace on those sleeves and a new straw bonnet with ribbon to match your dress!" Charlotte was feeling a twinge of jealousy.

Gilbert immediately jumped in and took Amy Ann by the arm.

"Please, allow me to escort you Ma'am," Gilbert teased her.

"Oh, Gilbert!" Amy Ann was embarrassed from all the attention and she pushed Gilbert away.

"Now, now, that's enough," cautioned Aunt Sarah. "Let's not make a fuss."

Charlotte suggested that they sit on the porch and relax. She explained that the meal wasn't quite ready and they were still setting the table. Aunt Sarah was just fine with that. She took a seat in the rocking chair and Amy Ann sat on the porch bench.

It wasn't long before everyone was called in to eat and a prayer was said. Henry ate out on the porch as Aunt Sarah directed. Everyone seemed to be enjoying the meal and company of one another. Even Aunt Sarah was engaged in enjoyable conversation. The subject soon turned to the yearly barn dance and pig roast that would follow the coming harvest in late October. The Donaldsons would host the event this year as they did every year. The ladies made plans of what they would cook and bake for the event.

Following the meal Aunt Sarah bragged on Cora's good cooking.

"Thank you, Miss Sarah," said Cora. "Gilbert was a big help, too. I couldn't have done it without him."

Oliver and S.W. agreed that the meal was exceptional. Betsy and Adaline bragged on the fine cooking and all the hard work that Cora did to prepare it. Gilbert sneaked on outside along with Oliver and sat on the back porch with Henry. Gilbert enjoyed talking to Henry about Ohio River life in East Liverpool and Gilbert hoped that someday Henry would tell him his secrets and how he came to be with Aunt Sarah.

S.W. was glad to spend the afternoon with Adaline even though he had to share her company. He worried that Adaline might be upset that Cora was living with them, although Adaline never made mention of it. S.W. and Adaline took advantage of sitting on the front porch since it wasn't occupied. After engaging in some casual conversation S.W. gazed into Adaline's soft brown eyes, his pulse quickened, and he said, "You know I love you, Adaline. It hasn't been easy for me to tell you with everybody around." He briefly mentioned the rumors of war and that he might be expected to enlist should war break out with the South.

She looked in his eyes and said, "I dare say, I am surprised and sorry... to think that ye being a Christian would ever consider going off to war. Tis only hearsay... the war I mean. I shan't bear to hear of it."

He held on to both of her hands and leaned forward to gently kiss her. At that exact moment, Henry came around the corner of the house and witnessed the entire event. Henry winked and grinned at S.W. as he went on around the house then S.W. quickly kissed her again.

"Ye know, I love ye, too," Adaline whispered. She longed for the day when they would marry. She abruptly jumped up and returned inside the house.

Amy Ann was drying the dishes when Adaline stepped in to help. "I saw him kiss you," Amy Ann whispered in Adaline's ear. She took delight in teasing her.

Adaline was embarrassed as she grabbed a towel to help dry the dishes.

Her sister Betsy gave her a stern look of disapproval and angrily said, "Tis 'bout time ye came back in to help!"

Adaline paid no attention to Betsy. She continued drying the last of the dishes and then sat down at the table with Amy Ann.

Aunt Sarah was supervising the cleanup when she noticed that Cora was looking very pale.

"Oh my dear, you are looking a little peaked. Why don't you go out and get some fresh air?"

Cora responded, "Oh, thank you, Miss Sarah, I think I will

sit on the porch for a spell. I do need some fresh air." Cora took a towel with her to wipe the perspiration from her face. She was feeling very warm and a little dizzy. Aunt Sarah sat with her on the porch.

"My dear, perhaps it is time for you to return with me and see the doctor?"

"Oh, no Miss Sarah, I'll be fine. I'd like to stay awhile longer to help out and maybe attend the barn dance. That is if you don't mind my staying?" Cora tried to be cheerfully convincing.

"Well, my dear, if you think you feel up to it."

Aunt Sarah took a look around to make sure they were indeed alone on the porch and no one could hear their conversation.

"I received a letter from the lawyer in Cincinnati regarding the settlement of Mrs. Johnson's estate. There is an investigation taking place as to the rightful ownership." Aunt Sarah was standing very close to Cora speaking in a very low tone when Gilbert surprisingly came around the house and stepped up onto the porch.

"Hello Gilbert, would you mind getting us a cold drink from the well?" Aunt Sarah smiled at him. She was waving the towel like a fan to cool Cora's face.

"Why are you waving that towel? Is Cora sick?" Gilbert questioned.

"Oh, I just got a little over heated in the kitchen. Some cold water would really taste good," Cora explained.

"Sure thing, I won't be long." Gilbert went on the run with a bucket in his hand to get water.

Aunt Sarah quickly continued, "Cora, come into town the first chance you get so we can discuss this in private. You can see the doctor then, too."

Cora agreed to do as Aunt Sarah suggested. Cora was excited and very much wanted to read the contents of the letter. Gilbert was back in a flash with the water so any additional information that Aunt Sarah had to share came to a halt.

"Here's the water! I'll get you a mug! I'll get one of those Rockingham mugs!" Gilbert ran into the kitchen.

"Cora, I do hope you will come to my place soon." Aunt Sarah sat on the porch bench and waited on Gilbert to return to dip the water from the bucket.

The afternoon had proven to be eventful. Now, it was time for everyone to say their goodbyes and return home. Aunt Sarah was the first to depart, but it took some encouragement to get S.W. to hitch up the horse and take Adaline and Betsy home. He made sure it was a slow ride back to the Truby place, however, with Betsy along he wasn't free to speak from his heart to Adaline.

Cora went to bed early. It was the first time she had gone

to bed early since her arrival there. She could hear Charlotte and Amy Ann talking about what a wonderful day it had been. It made Cora feel good to know they were happy as they had come to be like family to her.

Chapter Seven
Late October 1860
Kalida, Ohio

Cora went to visit Aunt Sarah regarding the matter of Mrs. Johnson's estate. An investigation was underway as to the rightful ownership of the property. Other information was not disclosed except that a lawyer from Cincinnati would be contacting Aunt Sarah in the near future. Cora visited the doctor as Aunt Sarah had suggested. Aunt Sarah prepared a room for Cora at her place in anticipation of her moving back in soon.

Summer came to an end and folks were getting ready for another cold northwestern Ohio winter. Folks would be slowing down a bit once the crops were all harvested.

Now was the time for Charlotte and Amy Ann to go with Aunt Sarah to visit the grave of their older sister, Hannah. They still grieved over her unexpected death following the birth of her third child. She was only twenty-four at the time of her death on May 8, 1859. They would stop by to visit with Hannah's widower and their three children. He had remarried and they wanted to meet his new wife. It was a difficult visit and Amy Ann and Charlotte were sad.

"Aunt Sarah... the children don't remember us." Amy Ann solemnly remarked on their ride home.

Aunt Sarah commented, "Life isn't always easy. Just be thankful for what we have."

Sadness overshadowed their journey home and the silence of unspoken words expressed their sorrow.

The month of October brought more excitement to Perry Township. Talk of the upcoming election and a possible Southern rebellion was causing a stir. Election Day, November 6th, would soon prompt folks into action.

Cora stayed on to help for a little while longer. She didn't talk much and it was apparent she wasn't feeling well. S.W. still thought there was something amiss about Cora and he wished that he could figure it out. He still had a hard time keeping his eyes off her and for that he was ashamed. There were times when he thought she might have the same thoughts about him, though he knew better than to explore any such feelings. His heart belonged to Adaline.

It was Wednesday, October 31st and Gilbert had been a gadabout all day and now that it was dark he was nowhere to be found.

"It's getting late. Does anyone know where Gilbert is?" Charlotte anxiously asked.

"I'm sure he's fine. Don't worry, he'll be home soon." Cora tried to be reassuring.

"Well, he's always home by dark." Charlotte paced the floor and looked out the front door for any signs of a lantern light on the road.

"I'll ride over to the Donaldsons'. They might know where he is." S.W. tried to sound encouraging.

"I'll go with you," said Oliver.

They hitched up the horse and buggy. In just a short time they were knocking on the Donaldsons' front door. Mr. Donaldson came to the door and shined a lantern on the porch.

"What are you fellas doing out at this hour?"

"We were wondering if you've seen Gilbert? He's been gone all day and never came home this evening," Oliver explained.

Mr. Donaldson poked his head back inside the house and asked, "Any of you young'uns seen Gilbert?"

"No, Pappy! We saw him yesterday. He was talking about visiting with Old Dan," Ben reported. Ben was the same age as Gilbert; he and Gilbert were friends.

"Are you sure that's all you know? His family is on the hunt of him. You boys best be tellin' the truth."

"We are truthful, Pappy. All Gilbert talks about are those Wide Awakes and how he wants to go meet up with them. That's all we know," said Ben.

"Can we go hunt for him?" one of the younger children yelled out. Mr. Donaldson ignored the young child's request and went out on the porch. He turned the lantern up. The whole front porch was bright with light. Oliver and S.W. could clearly be seen dressed in warm wool winter coats which came just above their knees. Their neck scarves were wrapped around their ears and necks. Their black slouch hats were pulled down.

"You heard what the young'uns said. Best take a look at Old Dan's place."

"Thanks. Sorry for bothering you," said Oliver.

"No bother. Gilbert's most likely with Old Dan. You fellas be careful travelin' in the dark. Here, you better take this lantern."

"Thanks again," said S.W. as he took the lantern from Mr. Donaldson.

"Well, Old Dan might shoot us if we go knocking on his door in the middle of the night," said S.W. as they got back in the buggy.

"It should be alright to approach the old man's place," Oliver reasoned, "He knows us."

"I bet Gilbert took off for one of those Wide Awakes'

meetings," assumed S.W.

"Why would you say that?" Oliver questioned.

"He's been carrying a newspaper notification around in his pocket for months. I didn't think he was serious," said S.W.

"Old Dan is quite the storyteller. If a young boy listens to him long enough he might try to join up. We could be traveling to Toledo or Fort Wayne to find him," speculated Oliver.

"Gilbert wouldn't just take off on his own. He has never journeyed far from home," said S.W.

"Well, here we are at Old Dan's. No lights in the cabin or in the barn," said Oliver.

"I can hear the dog barking." S.W. made a gesture toward the barn.

"We better go knock at the cabin first. He could be asleep," said Oliver as he jumped down from the buggy. S.W. was right behind him with the lantern. They banged hard on the door and called out his name, but there was no answer. The dog continued to bark from inside the barn.

"Let's go to the barn. He might be there?" considered S.W.

Oliver opened the barn door and yelled, "Dan! Dan! You in there? It's Oliver and S.W.! We come looking for Gilbert!"

The long-haired sable collie came to the barn door to greet them. Oliver opened the door wider and peered through the darkness of the barn.

"Bring the lantern closer," commanded Oliver. "There he

is passed out with a jug of whiskey."

Oliver entered the barn. Oliver knelt on his knees to grab hold of the old man's shoulders in an attempt to waken him. Old Dan was in a drunken sleep.

"You mean empty jug. Here's a crate hidden in the hay." S.W. moved the hay back so he could read the label. "Old Style Kentucky brand whiskey. He's got quite a stash here. I never would've thought it."

"Let's get him back to the cabin and put some coffee down him. It's too cold out here for the old man," Oliver declared as he got under his arms and dragged him out the door.

The collie stayed close by and followed them into the cabin. A few dying embers glowed in the fireplace. The cabin was cold. The collie remained by Old Dan's side. Oliver laid Dan on the bed and the collie lay on the floor beside him.

"I'll gather some firewood and warm this place up." S.W. went back outside to the wood pile and quickly packed in a stack of wood.

It took a while for the cabin to get warm and to make the coffee. They were finally able to rouse Old Dan. His speech was a bit slurred even after drinking coffee and having a bite to eat. He told them that Gilbert had intentions of meeting a man at McClure's General Store and joining him on a trip to Toledo.

"Do you know the man's name?" questioned Oliver.

"No, can't say that I do. He said something about Summit Street in Toledo and fireworks. That's all I recall." Old Dan was warmed by the fire and was sobering up when he added, "Oh, and he wanted to see the parade."

"Thanks, Dan. We got to get home." Oliver and S.W. put on their coats and bundled up.

"No sense chasing after the boy tonight. He's long gone," said Old Dan.

"You be right about that," replied Oliver. "Take it easy on the whiskey. One of these days we're going to find you dead as a doornail."

"Whiskey is what keeps me going! How do ya think I lived this long?" Old Dan chuckled.

"Goodnight, Dan," said S.W. and Oliver as they went out the door. The horse and buggy was tied to the porch post. They climbed in the buggy and slowly headed home in the darkness.

It was very late when Oliver and S.W. arrived home, but Charlotte, Cora, and Amy Ann were waiting up. Cora was sitting by the fireplace crocheting. Charlotte was sitting at the table weaving a small basket while Amy Ann handed her the water soaked wooden reeds from a tub of water. A lantern sat in the middle of the table where they were working. The room was well lit. Oliver and S.W. came in through the backdoor.

"Is Gilbert with you?" Charlotte was excited and hoping that he would be coming through the door with them.

"No, Old Dan said he went to Toledo with some fella that he met up with at McClure's store." Oliver removed his coat, hat, and scarf. He hung it up on a wooden peg on the log wall.

"Why ever would he go off with a stranger?" Charlotte stood up and wiped her hands on her apron. "Are you going after him?"

"We're going in the morning. We don't know the fella, but most likely Mr. McClure does," said S.W. "Hopefully Mr. McClure can give us some information."

"You girls will be alright for a couple of days. If you should need anything the Trubys will help." Oliver instructed.

"Just find Gilbert!" Charlotte sobbed.

"Why ever would Gilbert want to go to Toledo? I don't understand," said Cora.

"There's plenty of activity there and lots of excitement," explained Oliver. "Gilbert is looking for excitement. The whole country is caught up in the excitement of the election."

"Yes, and Gilbert has a newspaper notification of the Wide Awakes and their meetings," S.W. further explained. "There is to be a grand celebration. Everyone says that Abraham Lincoln will be our President."

"I'm really worried about Gilbert," said Amy Ann. She was crying as she climbed the steps to the loft.

When daybreak appeared, Oliver and S.W. headed to McClure's General Store. Mr. McClure was sitting by the woodstove reading the newspaper from Toledo when S.W. and Oliver walked in.

"Ye fellas is up mighty early. What can I do for ye?" Mr. McClure rubbed his eyes in an effort to wake up.

"Good morning, Mr. McClure," said S.W. as he and Oliver walked back to join him by the warmth of the stove. The store smelled of wood and tobacco smoke. The smoke lingered in the air. The light from the lantern was dim. A coffee pot was steaming on top the stove.

"Gilbert never came home last night. We were at Old Dan's late last night looking for him. Dan claims that Gilbert has been hanging out with some fella that stops by here from time-to-time," Oliver earnestly inquired. "We thought you might have some information for us to go on."

"There was a fella come in here a day ago, said he come from Fort Wayne and was goin' to Toledo and might go on up to Saginaw. Gilbert was here then," said Mr. McClure. He stood up to put another piece of wood in the stove. He poked at the hot ashes to get the wood to burn faster. More smoke escaped when Mr. McClure opened the stove door and red hot ashes fell in the ash pan.

Mr. McClure continued, "He be the same fella that come by here 'bout July or August. Said he was scoutin' for work and was a headin' north to Michigan. Fella was alone on horseback then. Now he's got a covered wagon. Reckon he found a good payin' job."

Mr. McClure went over to the counter and picked up a newspaper and handed it to Oliver. "Fella left this paper behind. He said folks might find it entertainin'."

Oliver silently read the paper in the faintly lit room and then said, "This is a public invitation. The Toledo Wide Awakes will have a grand meeting over the recent elections."

"Gilbert must've took it as a personal invite," said Mr. McClure. "Fella said he was settin' off for Toledo. I reckon Gilbert climbed in the wagon and went along. They ain't too far ahead. Can't go fast in a covered wagon."

"Thanks, Mr. McClure. We best be on our way," said Oliver.

Mr. McClure followed them out onto the porch as they were leaving.

"Ye got good weather for travelin'." Mr. McClure stood on the porch looking at the sky. "Be seein' ye lads in a few days." Mr. McClure stood on the porch in the cold morning air with his arms folded.

Oliver and S.W. stepped down off the porch and Oliver untied the horse.

"Ye lads do know that Toledo is a big town? Best keep an eye open and watch ye pockets. Too bad ye can't take the Stage or the train, except then ye couldn't be a trailin' the boy."

"Much obliged to you, Mr. McClure," said Oliver.

S.W. and Oliver climbed into the enclosed buggy and started out on a cold journey north. They would stay overnight at the Stagecoach Inn before reaching Toledo.

Oliver and S.W. traveled at a steady pace for about ten miles until they reached a small dwelling in the woods. A creek was nearby with a footpath leading to it. It would be easy to unhitch the horse and lead it down the narrow trail to water. As they were watering the horse they could hear someone chopping and splitting wood. Suddenly the sound ceased and a young boy about eight years of age appeared running towards them. An older man slowly walked behind the boy. The older man was short of breath when he met up with them, although the young boy was full of energy as was the beagle pup that trailed in behind him.

"Howdy," said the man as he caught up with them. "Please excuse the young'un. He gets mighty excited when folks stop by here. My name's Joseph Potts." He offered his hand.

"I'm Oliver Jeffrey and this is my brother S.W." Oliver and S.W. shook hands with Mr. Potts and the young boy.

"My name's Tom," said the boy and then he quickly asked, "where you fellas headed?"

"Toledo," answered S.W.

"Mama says that's a far piece, cause that's where she's from."

"Now son, that will be enough. Might be that these fellas

would like to join us for a bite to eat and rest for a spell?"

"Well... sir... if it's not too much trouble? It would be nice to sit for a spell," Oliver replied.

"Not at all. We can take your horse and buggy to the barn," said Mr. Potts. "The Mrs. will be glad for the company."

"Tom, go tell your Mama we got company." The young boy ran to the cabin.

S.W. and Oliver found the small cabin to be warm and it smelled of fresh baked bread. Mrs. Potts was busy preparing the table for the noonday meal. Mr. Potts introduced S.W. and Oliver to Mrs. Potts and they all sat down at the table. Mrs. Potts filled their bowls with stew from a pot on the stove and passed the bread and butter around the table. The warmth of the cabin and the food was relaxing. Mr. Potts was right, Mrs. Potts enjoyed their company, in addition to being most informative about Toledo.

"Toledo," she paused for a moment and smiled, "Toledo is my home town. I was born and raised there." She proceeded to fill their minds with images of what the town must be like. "Oh, there is so much building and construction in Toledo. There are thousands of people there now and more are coming."

"Mama, how many people live there?"

"Oh, I would say about ten thousand or maybe more," she answered.

"Now, now, Tom, no more questions. Allow our guests to eat their meal. I'm sure they want to head out soon," said Mr. Potts.

"As a matter of fact, we are in a hurry. You see we are searching for our little brother, Gilbert. He's fourteen. We're pretty sure he took off with a fella in a covered wagon. We think Gilbert intends to meet up with the Wide Awakes in Toledo."

"Mr. Owens and Gilbert were here yesterday!" exclaimed little Tom.

"Hush, now boy!" ordered Mr. Potts. The boy hung his head in disappointment.

"Yes, Mr. Owens was here yesterday and Gilbert was with him. He sure never acted like he was running away or anything was wrong," said Mrs. Potts.

"Would you be so kind as to tell us where we might locate Mr. Owens?" Oliver was truly provoked.

"Mr. Owens will be stoppin' in Toledo for a couple of days. Then he will be movin' up north," interjected Mr. Potts. "He claims to have work in Michigan."

"Would you know exactly where in Toledo we might find Mr. Owens? We only want to get Gilbert back home as soon as we can." Oliver's voice sounded stern.

"Well, if you go to the east edge of town you'll find a livery stable. That's most likely where he will take his team and pitch camp in a nearby field. That's where most folks join up with the wagon train," reasoned Mr. Potts.

Oliver and S.W. excused themselves from the table and expressed their gratitude. When Oliver stood up to retrieve his coat and hat he noticed a book on the mantel above the fireplace. Mrs. Potts was closely watching his expression as he glanced at a book.

"Have you had the pleasure of reading it?" inquired Mrs. Potts. The book on the mantel was Uncle Tom's Cabin.

"No, Ma'am, I don't have the time to read much. I'm right sure it's most interesting."

"It highlights the evils of slavery. How do you regard runaway slaves?"

"I'm more concerned about our runaway brother," said Oliver very gruffly.

"Rightly so and you should be. Good luck to you," replied Mrs. Potts.

Mr. Potts walked with them to the barn to help with their horse and buggy.

"You fellas should be able to reach the Stagecoach Inn before nightfall. That is if you travel at a steady pace." Mr. Potts was helping harness the horse. "Now remember, you're welcome to stop here on your way back through. You can stop here anytime."

"We're much obliged to you and your wife. We'll be seeing

you," replied Oliver.

"Many thanks to you and Mrs. Potts," said S.W. as he climbed into the buggy.

They had traveled another ten or twelve miles when the sun was just starting to set and they came upon the road signs pointing to the Stagecoach Inn.

"Mr. Potts was right," said Oliver. "There's the sign for the Stagecoach Inn. It's just a few miles ahead." They arrived at the Inn just as it was getting dark.

The tavern was busy. It was a regular stop for stage lines running to Toledo, Ohio, and Detroit, Michigan. Some of the passengers who were traveling to Toledo by stage reported they wanted to get there before the huge crowd gathered for the rally that was expected to fill the streets.

S.W. and Oliver decided they had better stay at the Inn for the night and get an early start in the morning.

They entered the livery stable and gave their horse and buggy over for safe keeping. They questioned the livery keeper about Mr. Owens and any other details he might remember.

"Well, let me see now. My memory don't always serve me right," said the old livery keeper. He rubbed his chin and adjusted his hat. He went about scooping feed from a barrel and pouring it into the feed boxes in each of the stalls. His teeth were tobacco stained and some teeth were noticeably missing. He leaned against the stall and proceeded to speak.

"As near as I can recall... Gilbert did lots of complainin'. The man said he was 'bout ready to leave him behind. He was tired of listenin' to him whine."

He continued to scoop feed from the barrel and into the feed boxes. The only sound in the stables was that of the horses chewing grain. The old man spit tobacco juice and continued chewing with his jaw protruding from the wad of tobacco.

"Thanks, Mister. I reckon we can catch up with the wagon tomorrow. We heard he might be going to the livery stable on the east edge of town," said Oliver.

"That sounds 'bout right," the old livery keeper agreed. "That be where folks set up camp... on the east edge of town."

"Then we can locate Gilbert and that fella he's with," Oliver angrily concluded.

"You best leave early in the mornin' if you're a stayin' the night in Toledo," the livery keeper chided in. "That is if you want to get a room."

"Thanks, old timer. We will be up early to get the horse and buggy," replied Oliver.

"I'll be right here," he said and spit tobacco juice on the ground.

Oliver and S.W were up early just as they planned. They had a big breakfast at the Inn and then headed for the livery stable. The old man had their horse and buggy ready to go.

They paid him for the care of their horse and bid the old man farewell.

Chapter Eight
Toledo, Ohio

The morning air was cool and crisp. It looked like it might rain. Oliver and S.W worried that the rain would slow them down and they might not reach Toledo by nightfall. S.W. and Oliver were relieved to see the clouds rolling on with no rain in sight.

At the east edge of town, they easily located the livery stable. The livery keeper pointed out the camp sites in the field nearby. There were several covered wagons all with campfires and lanterns lit for the night. A corral was roped off for the horses to graze. The livery keeper didn't know which wagon belonged to Mr. Owens.

"Well, you fellers will just have ta' go down thar' and inquire on yar' own. Somebody will point 'em out to ya." The livery keeper led them to the path leading to the camp.

S.W. and Oliver took long strides following the path and stopped at the first campfire. The family sitting around the fire didn't know Mr. Owens, although a new wagon had joined up this morning. All of the wagons were headed north to Michigan where work was reported to be plentiful. Another wagon train was forming in the outer field. This wagon train was heading west to Chicago, Illinois. The family had been kind enough to share all the information they knew, however any information leading them to Gilbert was to no avail.

S.W. and Oliver proceeded to walk around the camp until they came to the wagon thought to belong to Mr. Owens. A fire was blazing in the fire ring making visible a large area near the wagon. Mr. Owens was sitting just outside of the wagon on an old chair he had brought along. He was smoking a long stem pipe.

Oliver spoke first. "Good evening. Might you be Mr. Owens?"

"That be me, alright. And who might you be?" He asked as he got up from his chair. He appeared to be a much larger man when he stood up. He looked like a strong, stout, and robust man.

"I'm Oliver Jeffrey and this is my brother S.W."

"Oh... would you be trailing after Gilbert? He set off, not too long ago. He said he was looking for the convention hall up on Summit Street. He wants to get in line for the parade and listen to the brass band. You might say he's of a determined nature." Mr. Owens took a draw on his pipe. "He's dead set on joining those Wide Awakes!"

Oliver took a few steps closer. He was so close that a breeze wafted pipe smoke in his eyes.

"What have you to say for yourself, taking Gilbert along with you on this journey? Did not you think he had a family that would come looking for him?" Oliver demanded an answer.

"Now see here... I didn't force Gilbert to come along. The lad offered to pay his way and said he'd be getting off in Toledo. He's plenty old enough to travel on his own," declared Mr. Owens.

"I can't reason why you fellas would be making such a fuss over the lad? Why he must be right near sixteen or seventeen? He's big and strong as an ox. He can take care of himself."

"You need not encourage a boy to go off roaming about the country on his own. His sisters are worried sick over him and we have been traveling two days searching for him!" Oliver yelled at Mr. Owens.

"Well there's nothing I can do about that! You best go on up to Summit Street and find your... little... brother!" shouted angry Mr. Owens. The large, bearded, lumberjack type of a man laid his pipe on the chair preparing for a fist fight.

"I see no need to fight over this," said S.W. as he stepped closer to Mr. Owens. "We're wasting time here." He glanced at Oliver.

"I reckon you're right. Let's go," replied Oliver.

"Good luck finding him in that rowdy crowd!" Mr. Owens sat back down in his old chair and continued smoking his pipe. He watched Oliver and S.W. walk the path leading to the town.

The town lights could be seen in the distance. Oliver and S.W. hadn't anticipated the busy streets and brightly decorated buildings. Residences were brightly lighted along the streets and banners were stretched out high across the streets connected to lamp posts and rooftops. The banners were written with bold lettering... Lincoln & Hamlin. Oliver and S.W. walked down Elm Street and when they came to Cherry Street they could hear the band playing as the procession marched toward them.

"The streets are crowded! There must be hundreds of people here tonight!" S.W. had to shout above the sound of the brass band.

The crowd was singing Lincoln's campaign song, Lincoln and Liberty; Hurrah for the choice of the nation! The singing got louder as more people joined in.

"We better make our way to Summit Street and locate the convention hall! Maybe someone there can help us!" Oliver said as he nudged his way through the crowd.

"Look there, just ahead! That's Lily Baramore! Remember, I told you about her?" S.W. put his hand on Oliver's shoulder to stop him and pointed Lily out in the crowd. "Might be she could help us!" Now they found it even more difficult to get through the crowd. Lily was standing with a very well dressed group of people.

"Miss Baramore! Miss Baramore! Lily!" S.W. attempted to yell out above the noise of the crowd.

"Oh, Lily, I do think someone is trying to get your attention. Look over there," said one of her friends pointing in S.W.'s direction.

"Well, that's a dear friend of mine! You don't mind if they join us, do you?"

"Of course not, any friend of yours, Lily, is welcome," replied her friend. All of her companions agreed and Lily motioned for S.W. and Oliver to join them. She waved her hands in the air in excitement. The whole atmosphere was filled with excitement. The fireworks were just beginning causing more havoc in the crowd.

Suddenly there was a lull in the crowd enabling S.W. and Oliver to get through. S.W. introduced Oliver and Lily tried to introduce her friends, except the noise was too much. Lily grabbed hold of S.W.'s arm and guided him along. Oliver somehow managed to keep up with them.

"We are on our way to a party! Please join us! There are so many people I want you to meet! This is such a joyful celebration and now that my old friend is here it is even more joyful!" Lily was excitedly trying to be heard above the crowd.

"Oh, come with us!" S.W. and Oliver found themselves being tugged along by Lily and her enthusiastic friends. "Oh, I wish Samuel had come along too!"

S.W. and Oliver followed Lily and her group of friends down Cherry Street to Summit Street, past brightly lit businesses and residences. S.W. and Oliver hadn't expected such a crowd. He knew this was not the time or place to ask about Gilbert. He hoped that the place where she was taking them would be more suitable to inquire of Gilbert's whereabouts. Finally, they stood on the front porch of a massive and eloquent brick home. They were greeted at the door by Mrs. Ash and promptly invited in. A house servant helped them with their coats. The group that was with Lily set out for the music room and joined in some lively singing.

Oliver whispered to S.W. "I don't think we're dressed for this social occasion. We best state what we're here for and go."

"Miss Lily, you have brought guests with you?" Mrs. Ash inquired of Lily.

"Why yes, I have. This is my friend S.W. and his brother Oliver Jeffrey. S.W. bravely came to my rescue when I was in Ottawa on business. I believe I told you about that encounter."

"Yes, I remember. So, very glad to make your acquaintance. I'm Mrs. Ash," she presented her white laced gloved hand to S.W.

He wasn't sure what to do with her hand so he reached out

and gently held her hand and bowed his head to her.

"A pleasure to meet you ma'am."

When Mrs. Ash offered her hand to Oliver he followed suit.

"My husband is at the convention hall attending to the many speakers and guests that are present tonight. I doubt that he will be home soon, however you are welcome to join us and stay as long as you like. We are always pleased to have new members for the Republican Party."

Quickly she turned to speak to Lily. "Oh, Lily, do show the gentlemen where the food and drinks are and introduce them to the others who have joined our rally for Lincoln."

"You are much too kind Mrs. Ash. At most, we are here in search of our brother, Gilbert. We would very much like directions to the convention hall. We think that might be where Gilbert is," explained S.W.

"Oh, it is much too crowded to ever find your brother tonight. What is the urgency?" Mrs. Ash asked.

"Well you see he is only a boy and his sisters are very concerned that he might join up with the Wide Awakes and not return home."

"I understand. Are not his parents also concerned?" she asked.

"Our parents are no longer with us," replied S.W.

"I'm very sorry to hear that. I know you are distressed. I

will send my servant with you to guide you through the busy streets to the hall."

Then Mrs. Ash instructed a gangly young servant, "Find Mr. Ash and tell him I sent you. Explain that these two men are looking for their young brother. Have Mr. Ash look in the registry book for new enlistments." And then she added, "Rush back as soon as you can. There is much work to be done here."

"Very well, ma'am. Just as you wish," replied the young house servant.

S.W. and Oliver expressed their gratitude. "Thank you Ma'am, you're very kind. We are indebted to you."

"Once you have found your brother, please come back and join us. I very much would like to meet your brother," Mrs. Ash demanded.

"I'll get your coats and see you out," said Lily.

Once they were at the door, Lily reminded them to be sure to return to the party. "Mrs. Ash will be most disappointed if you don't stop back and I will be disappointed too." She smiled her dimpled smile and flashed her snappy brown eyes as they departed.

The house servant certainly knew his way around the Toledo streets and back alleys. They were able to avoid much of the crowd. They came through the alley and entered the back of the large brick convention building. The young servant had to persuade the guard to let them enter. Once inside it was difficult to find Mr. Ash as the members were gathered to publicly express their views and exchange ideas. The speaker could be heard loudly proclaiming, "There will be no lack of soldiers. We will not back down. We the people of Northwestern Ohio will organize and be prepared to fight."

The house servant, now acting as their guide, pushed on through the hallway and continued to where Mr. Ash was congregating with other members.

"There is Mr. Ash. Follow me and I will introduce you," said the young servant.

"Mr. Ash, Sir, pardon the interruption, but Mrs. Ash has requested that you help these two gentlemen. They are friends of Miss Baramore. They are searching for their younger brother. They have reason to think he has recently enlisted with the Wide Awakes."

"Whatever can I do? If a lad wants to enlist I haven't the power to stop him." Mr. Ash glared at S.W. and Oliver.

"Sir, perhaps he isn't old enough to join? Mrs. Ash has asked that you please hear the men out."

"Very well, let us go where it is quiet." They followed him into a small chamber away from all the clamor. He opened the registry book and turned to the most recent page.

"What is your brother's name?" He was gruff.

"Gilbert Jeffrey," answered Oliver.

"No, no such name has been entered," said Mr. Ash as he glanced over the page.

"Perhaps it wasn't today. Could you look at yesterday's entries?" Oliver pleaded with the gruff Mr. Ash.

"This page contains the entire week. I am sorry. His name has not been entered." Mr. Ash closed the large thick book.

"Thank you, Mr. Ash. Thank you for your time and patience," said S.W.

"Very well... sorry you didn't find what you were looking for. I really must get back to my guests." Mr. Ash was curt.

S.W. spoke to the young servant, "We need to go back to thank Lily and Mrs. Ash before we leave."

"You had better stay with me or you will have a very difficult time finding your way back," suggested the young house servant. "I know some of the establishments that young men frequent. We can go by the billiards hall on our way back. There are a couple of pubs where he might take refuge, especially if he looks older than he really is."

They briskly walked around the back of some of the buildings to avoid the rowdy crowd. It was getting near to eleven o'clock and they could hear fighting and profanity in the streets. The Douglas Democrat Party had planned a demonstration just before midnight. The rabble-rousers were succeeding at stirring up some of the crowd. Mostly drunken confrontations and fist fights erupted. Gun shots were heard, despite having seen no injuries.

"I sure hope Gilbert doesn't get caught up in all this!" Oliver said loudly.

"I hope he is smart enough not to get involved in drunken rivalry," S.W. replied.

The house servant led them away from the fighting and took a safer route back to the big brick house.

"I'm sorry, the streets are just too crowded to look for your brother. If you would like, I can take you around in the morning?" The young house servant offered his assistance.

"Yes, morning would be good. Sorry for all the trouble we've caused. We hope we didn't get you in too much trouble with the lady of the house. We will go back with you to explain and apologize," said Oliver.

"It's almost midnight. Perhaps it will be too late to approach Mrs. Ash with our apologies?" S.W. was fearful of making a late entrance.

"The party will come to an end right at midnight. I don't think the ladies have retired for the evening. They enjoy the musical entertainers that Mrs. Ash invited. The musical family of singers will be house guests for a week or two. Did you hear them singing when you entered the house?"

"I'm sorry we didn't get a chance to stay and hear them. We didn't come prepared to socialize," answered Oliver.

The servant continued, "They wrote Lincoln's campaign

song, Lincoln and Liberty. The marching band played it and the crowd was singing it tonight."

"I guess we just weren't paying much attention to the singing. We had a tough time getting through the crowd and keeping up with Miss Lily."

They walked at a faster pace to get back to the big house before midnight. The lights were still on and piano music and singing could be heard outside when they stepped up onto the porch. The house servant instructed S.W. and Oliver to use the front door. He would enter through the servant's entrance in the back of the house.

"Use the brass door knocker and rap loudly," he said.

It took three times rapping on the stained glass double doors before anyone would answer. Finally, Lily opened the door. She looked as radiant as ever.

"Oh, do come in." Lily welcomed them with a big smile. "Mrs. Ash has retired for the evening and Mr. Ash hasn't returned yet. You are most welcome to join us," she said as she took their coats. "Do tell me what happened. Did you have any luck or at least a lead in finding Gilbert?"

"No luck at all," replied S.W.

They stood by the entrance way by the coat rack with mirror discussing the events of the evening. Oliver could see in the mirror, the group that was gathered by the piano. He looked at his own reflection and realized his appearance was very poor. He was feeling weary and frustrated. A shave and a haircut as well as a good bath would make an improvement. Oliver, having ruled out that it was too late for that, decided to offer apologies.

"Miss Lily, you will excuse us if we don't join you and your company? S.W. and I are not dressed for such an occasion. We have been traveling for two days. We really just stopped in to thank you and Mrs. Ash," Oliver tried to explain.

"Oh, how thoughtless of me," said Lily. "I know you must be exhausted. I'll have the servant who helped you earlier find a room for you."

"No, we can find a room or bed down at the livery stable if we need to." S.W. tried to discourage her.

S.W. was surprised and glad when the young servant stepped back into the entrance way to make a suggestion.

"Ma'am, might I be so bold as to suggest that the gentlemen might feel more comfortable in the servants' quarters. They came unprepared to join the party, not to mention the long distance they have traveled."

"Nonsense, these are my friends. Surely there is an empty room in this big house," Lily demanded.

"Ma'am, with all due respect... all the guest rooms are filled."

"Miss Lily, we would be very grateful to stay in the servants' quarters." S.W. brought the subject to an end.

"Alright then... please make sure they are comfortable," Lily directed.

"Gentlemen, please come with me," said the servant.

They found the servants' quarters to be most acceptable. They were able to shave and clean up. It was more than they had expected. They were invited to come into the kitchen to eat and sit for awhile before going to bed. A few of the servants were still washing dishes and cleaning up from the party.

"I be Mrs. O'Brady and just who might ye be?" Mrs. O'Brady was a very plump full-figured woman. She was busy cleaning the kitchen.

"This is Oliver Jeffrey and his brother S.W. They will be staying the night." The house servant who guided them through the town informed Mrs. O'Brady.

"And just who gave ye the authority, Mr. Peabody, to invite them into me kitchen?"

"Please excuse Mrs. O'Brady, she takes her work very seriously. She is the head cook and a fine one, too."

"Now don't be a tryin' to butter me up. I ask... who's authority do ye have?"

"The authority of Miss Lily Baramore. They are friends of hers. There are no empty guest rooms and I offered the servants' quarters to them. Will that be to your liking, Mrs. O'Brady?"

"What makes ye friends with Miss Lily? Ye don't be lookin'

like her kind." She directed the question to Oliver.

"Miss Lily is actually my brother's friend. We're sorry to intrude. We will be leaving in the morning."

"We came here looking for our little brother, Gilbert," S.W. started to explain the situation.

"Gilbert... Gilbert Jeffrey, that be his name? Ye brother he be? He come sniffin' 'round here with me boy, Willy. That Gilbert is an ox. Does his stomach ever fill up? Me boy... Willy brought him 'round here. The two of 'em beggin' for food. Tis work they need be doin'... not beggin' for food!"

"Gilbert came here begging for food? When did you last see him?" Oliver asked.

"He come 'round here this mornin' with Willy. Willy knows when the food gets served 'round here. He's always a lookin' for a hand out. I slipped 'em a few biscuits and sausages after the meal was served. I could lose me job over this."

"Now, now, Mrs. O'Brady, you know that wouldn't happen to you. You're the best cook in town. They wouldn't let you go," said the young servant, Mr. Peabody.

"And ye be full of the old blarney. A Charmer ye be... Mr. Peabody." Mrs. O'Brady dried the last of the dishes and put them away.

"Mrs. O'Brady, where is your boy... Willy? Could be that Gilbert is still with him," said Oliver.

"We be stayin' at the boardin' house over on Elm St. It ain't much, but I keep a roof over our heads. That be more than some folks do." Mrs. O'Brady was hanging up her apron and getting ready to leave.

"Mrs. O'Brady, would you let us walk with you to your home? Might be that Gilbert is there or Willy could tell us where he went," requested Oliver.

"I'll just tag along, too," said the servant, Mr. Peabody. "Mrs. O'Brady, you don't want to be walking home alone on a night like tonight. It could be dangerous for you."

"Oh for goodness sakes, don't be a fussin' over me. Come along if ye be comin'... before it be gettin' any later."

Oliver, S.W., Mr. Peabody, and Mrs. O'Brady walked to the boarding house on Elm Street. There were still a few men that looked like the rough and tumble sort, rambling through the streets or just standing around in front of the taverns. Finally, they reached the boarding house. A sign was nailed to a post in the yard that read...

Nellie's Boardinghouse
Vacant Rooms

The boardinghouse appeared to be in need of some minor repairs, still it looked tidy and clean on the outside. They followed Mrs. O'Brady around to the back of the house.

"Now ye fellas keep it quiet and don't be a wakin' the other boarders." Mrs. O'Brady gave them warning.

When they came around the corner of the house Willy and Gilbert were sitting on the back steps. Gilbert immediately jumped up to run. Oliver was swift to catch him and threw him down on the ground. Gilbert tried to escape, only he was no match for Oliver. Oliver held him to the ground and tried to reason with him. Gilbert finally calmed down and Oliver released him.

"I be tellin' ye again... not to wake the others," Mrs. O'Brady ordered.

"Willy, ye come in the house. These fellas got business to 'tend to." Mrs. O'Brady put her hands on Willy's shoulders to encourage him to get in the house.

"Ma, I want to stay out here with me friend, Gilbert."

"Come in the house Willy and mind ye own business." Willy reluctantly went in the house, nevertheless he stayed near the door listening to their conversation.

Oliver, S.W., and Gilbert sat on the porch. Mr. Peabody lingered nearby leaning against the porch post. It took a little time to convince Gilbert to return home. Oliver stressed that Charlotte and Amy Ann would need a man around the place in case he and S.W. would be called away for awhile.

Gilbert didn't question him. He knew what Oliver was getting at. "I reckon you're right." That's all Gilbert had to say about the matter and he was ready to go.

Willy came back out onto the porch. "I reckon ye is needed

at home, Gilbert. Ye brother is right… ye got to stay with ye family.”

"Ahhh… I wish you could come along Willy.”

"And just who would be a helpin' ye poor old Ma?” Mrs. O'Brady was quick to question Willy when she came back outside.

Willy looked surprised and went to stand beside her.

"Well, Mrs. O'Brady we thank you for all your help. We'll be saying goodnight now… and again… thank you,” Oliver said with sincerity in his voice. He shook Mrs. O'Brady's hand before stepping down off the porch.

"Yes, a big thanks to you, Mrs. O'Brady, for helping us.” S.W. stepped down off the porch and Mr. Peabody followed.

Gilbert said goodbye to Willy and asked him to write to him. "Send your letter to the Franconia Post Office. I'll be lookin' for a note from you.”

Willy waved to them as they left and walked up the street. Mr. Peabody led the way back to the Ash residence and Gilbert questioned where Mr. Peabody was taking them.

"Do you remember me telling you about Miss Lily?” S.W. posed the question.

"I sure do!” Gilbert sounded excited.

"Well, this is your lucky night. You get to meet her.”

"Ahhh… you're just a joshin',” Gilbert responded.

"No, Gilbert, it's true. Mr. Peabody is taking us to the

Ash's house and Miss Lily is a guest there," said S.W.

"Why are we goin' there?" Gilbert was confused.

Mr. Peabody explained to Gilbert that they would be staying the night in the servants' quarters with him.

"There's a good chance that Miss Lily is still up. Lots of folks stay up past midnight on rally nights," Mr. Peabody speculated.

They arrived at the house and entered through the servant's door. Mr. Peabody showed them where they would be sleeping then he excused himself saying, "I hope you are able to get some rest tonight. I know you have a long journey ahead of you in the morning. You'll find soap and water on the washstand and towels hanging on the side bars. Goodnight to you all."

"Goodnight to you, Mr. Peabody and thank you," Oliver said as he sat down on the small cot to remove his boots and prepare for bed.

S.W. and Gilbert washed up in a hurry and didn't waste any time getting into bed.

The next morning, they were awakened by Mrs. O'Brady who was banging pots and pans around in the kitchen. Mr. Peabody was already up and dressed in his servant attire. He was in the kitchen helping Mrs. O'Brady prepare breakfast. Another younger woman had joined them in the kitchen to help with the cooking.

Oliver, S.W., and Gilbert quietly entered the kitchen so as not to disturb them while they worked. Mr. Peabody saw them and offered them seats at the servants' table.

"Sit here and have breakfast before you go." Mr. Peabody immediately filled three cups with coffee and placed a small pitcher of cream and a sugar bowl on the table.

"No, we must be on our way," Oliver put his hand in the air to stop the young servant from placing a plate of biscuits and butter on the table.

Mrs. O'Brady stopped what she was doing and turned around to face them. They were surprised to see how fast she could move her round plump body about the kitchen. Suddenly she stood before them with a large platter of sausages and eggs.

"Now, don't ye be refusin' the cook's food. That lad there, Gilbert, likes me cookin'." She set the platter down and demanded they take a seat.

They obeyed her and sat down at the breakfast feast. S.W. said a prayer of thanks and then they passed the platter around and loaded their plates with sausages and eggs.

"Do you think there's a chance we might get to see Miss Lily before we go?" Gilbert inquired.

Just then the kitchen door flung open and there stood Miss Lily. She was all smiles and bright eyed. She was wearing her dark blue night robe that tied in the front and her long dark hair flowed down her back.

"Good morning gentlemen. I'm so glad I found you. I'm pleased to see you are enjoying your breakfast." She sashayed over to the table where they were sitting and said, "I'm sorry I'm not formally dressed, but I wanted to see you before you left and I had to meet Gilbert."

Oliver, S.W., and Gilbert stood up to greet her. "Good morning," Oliver said and shook her hand. "We are very thankful to you and Mrs. Ash for letting us stay."

S.W. offered his hand and said, "Yes, indeed we are very thankful."

Miss Lily smiled approvingly and moved around the table to introduce herself to Gilbert.

"Gilbert, finally I get to meet you. I'm so glad you decided to visit Toledo. You are so brave to journey on your own." She shook hands with him. "Please, sit down and finish your breakfast." She sat down at the table beside Gilbert.

"It's nice to meet you too, Miss Lily. I mean Miss Baramore," Gilbert finally found his voice after he sat down.

"Oh, please call me Lily."

Mr. Peabody brought Miss Lily a cup of coffee and politely asked if she would be joining the gentlemen for breakfast or eating with the other guests.

"Oh, I would very much enjoy eating with these fine gentlemen. Thank you, Mr. Peabody." Miss Lily sat comfortably at the table. She poured cream in her coffee and asked S.W. to pass the sugar.

Mr. Peabody hurriedly gathered a plate and utensils for Miss Lily. "Will this be sufficient Miss Lily or can I get you anything else?"

"This will be just fine, Mr. Peabody... Thank you." Lily sipped on the very hot coffee.

"I don't know how you were able to find Gilbert in this crowded town, be that as it may, I'm so glad you did," Miss Lily reached for the butter dish and proceeded to place a small amount of butter on a biscuit. "Tell me Gilbert, how did you like the parade and big brass band?"

"I thought it was real nice! I never did see a brass band before and so many folks in the streets." Gilbert wiped his mouth with the cloth napkin that Mr. Peabody handed him. "Miss Lily, do you know that I play the fiddle and S.W. plays the mouth harp? We are pretty good at it, too."

"Why no, I had no idea S.W. could play the mouth harp and you play a fiddle. You must be keeping your talents a secret." She locked eyes with S.W. for a moment and smiled then continued talking. "I'd love to be entertained by you sometime. Perhaps we could arrange that when I come to visit your Aunt Sarah at Christmas time?"

"You know Aunt Sarah? She never mentioned you," Gilbert was quick to speak.

Miss Lily laughed at Gilbert's question. "Your Aunt Sarah was a very good friend to my mother... and my Papa. So, you see Gilbert, I've known your Aunt for a very long time." Miss Lily took a bite of biscuit and sipped more coffee before continuing her conversation.

"So, Gilbert, did you have a good time last night? Is Toledo everything you thought it would be?"

"It's alright," he said. "I'm sorry I didn't get to talk to any of the Wide Awakes or spend time with 'em." He sounded disappointed. "Their uniforms cost thirteen dollars and I didn't have the money for that!"

Lily sighed. "I suppose it's all for the best. I understand you're quite the man around home. Your sisters would miss having your help. I'm sure they love you very much."

"I suppose you're right." Gilbert loaded more eggs and sausages on his plate. He seemed to be more interested in food at the moment.

Miss Lily turned the conversation to Oliver. "So, Oliver, it would be so nice if you and your brothers would consider staying awhile longer. You are welcome to stay here. I'm sure Mr. and Mrs. Ash would agree." Miss Lily was anticipating getting to know them better.

Oliver gazed into her beautiful snappy brown eyes and said, "Your invitation is hard to resist. We do have responsibilities at home. I'm sorry we didn't get to see more of you and your friends."

Miss Lily immediately answered, "I'm sorry, too. Perhaps we could get together when I come to visit your aunt?" Lily kept her eyes on him as she waited for his answer.

Oliver agreed that such a visit might work out and he would be looking forward to it.

Gilbert chimed in with his thoughts on the matter. "Miss Lily, I'll make sure we're there! I can hardly wait!" Gilbert was just finishing off the last bite on his plate. His mouth was stuffed full of eggs and sausage.

S.W. sat silently listening to their plans to meet at Aunt Sarah's place at Christmas time. He thought it was another one of Miss Lily's schemes to recruit help for her anti-slavery cause, however he found himself agreeing to the meeting.

They said their farewells, gathered their warm wool frock coats, neck scarves, gloves and slouch hats, and made their way outside.

It was colder now and they were glad that Mr. Peabody had given them a couple of warm blankets to take with them on the journey back. Mrs. O'Brady had prepared a basket of food for their journey home. Miss Lily had seemed genuinely sad that they were leaving as she hugged each of them before they went out the door and reminded them once again of their meeting at Aunt Sarah's place.

Chapter Nine
Home at Last

$\mathcal{I}$t was two days traveling before they arrived back at the farm. Charlotte and Amy Ann heard the dogs barking and got up to see who was there. Gilbert ran into the house to get warm leaving S.W. and Oliver to take care of the horse and buggy. He was abruptly met at the door by Charlotte and Amy Ann who gave him hugs and kisses before proceeding to scold him for running off.

Gilbert ran over to stand in front of the fireplace. He stood there for a few minutes and then asked, "Where's Cora? Did she go off to bed early?"

"No, Gilbert, she went back to stay with Aunt Sarah." Charlotte didn't offer an explanation as to why.

"Well, I reckon I need to make a trip into town real soon to see her. Did she get to go to the hog roast and barn dance?" Gilbert sounded and looked real serious.

"No, Gilbert, she missed it and so did you, along with S.W.

and Oliver," Amy Ann responded with disappointment.

Oliver and S.W. entered the house in a hurry and picked up on the tail end of the conversation. "We missed the barn dance and hog roast because we were traipsing about the countryside looking for Gilbert," Oliver said with a hint of anger in his voice.

"Ahhh, I'm sorry! I really am. The first time I ever missed out on goin'." Gilbert took off his coat and winter clothing and laid it on a chair. He sat down by the fire and removed his boots to rub his cold feet.

S.W. walked over to sit by Gilbert in front of the fireplace. Oliver immediately washed up and went to bed.

Charlotte made a pot of piping hot tea and set out a plate of gingersnaps that she had made earlier in the day. Amy Ann wanted to know all the information they had to offer about their trip and finding Gilbert. Gilbert was most happy to tell the story and S.W. was willing to add a few more details of his own. They stayed up late into the night listening to S.W. and Gilbert give their accounts of the trip and tell of all the new folks they had met along the way including meeting up with Miss Lily once again.

The next day Oliver, S.W., and Gilbert all traveled in to McClure's General Store to get supplies. Several men were gathered around the old wood burning stove in the back of the store. As soon as they walked in the door Mr. McClure spoke up.

"Good mornin' to ye Gilbert. Tis surely good to see ye back home!" Mr. McClure patted Gilbert on the back as he walked by him.

Gilbert replied, "Thanks Mr. McClure. It's good to be home."

"Well, lad I been waitin' to hear all 'bout Toledo. Go on... ye ain't shy!" Mr. McClure said.

The men in the back of the store had stopped talking and were intently listening and waiting for Gilbert to speak.

"Oh, go on now Gilbert. We could do with some new tales around here," said Old Dan Sellers who was in the group of men standing around the stove.

"I think he's plumb tuckered out from the trip. I know I am," said Oliver as he walked across the old squeaky wooden floor to join the men. "Well, fellas, there's plenty of excitement in Toledo." Oliver picked up the broom and broke off a straw to chew on as he continued talking. "It's just like those stories and pictures in the newspaper about those Wide Awakes and their rallies. Only thing is... there's a lot more folks in Toledo than I ever dreamed. The whole town was crowded! Folks gathered in the streets to watch the parade."

"It's just like I told ya... ain't it? Did ya see the parade?" Old Dan was getting excited. He took a few puffs on his old long stemmed tobacco pipe. Pipe smoke lifted into the air and floated toward the ceiling. Dan sat straddled on an old ladderback chair with his arms resting over the back of the chair and his pipe in one hand.

"Old Dan, in the short time I was there I think I walked from one end of that town to the other and back again… thanks be to Gilbert." Oliver looked at Gilbert and chuckled.

Gilbert didn't think Oliver was very funny. "You know if it weren't for me you would've never seen the likes of Toledo and met up with Miss Lily!"

"Ye be right 'bout that, Gilbert," said Mr. McClure as he put a few more pieces of wood in the stove. "I heard 'bout Miss Lily." Mr. McClure shut the stove door and stood up tall. "I heard she be real purdy and a right clever woman, anyhow if she ain't careful… one day she could meet up with some real danger. Ye know what I mean?"

"Ahhh… Miss Lily is real nice. She won't meet up with no harm!" Gilbert was defensive. "Who would want to hurt her?"

"Ya never can tell, some folks is plumb crazy," said Old Dan. The other men mumbled in agreement.

S.W. stood waiting in the front of the store. He leaned against the wooden glass enclosed case that contained some fresh baked items and fresh eggs that one of the local women had brought in. "Do you reckon a fella could get waited on before Election Day gets here?" S.W. jokingly said and he grinned from ear-to-ear at Mr. McClure.

"Sure thing, S.W., ye be wantin' to purchase some a Mrs. Miller's baked goods?" Mr. McClure wiped his hands on his apron and walked back up front.

"I do!" Gilbert hustled to the front of the store to take a look at the sweets. "You got anymore hard candy in the tin boxes?"

"Not today, Gilbert. What else can I get ye?" Mr. McClure stared at S.W. and Gilbert waiting for an answer.

S.W. handed him a short list of items and Gilbert continued looking in the glass case trying to make a decision. Oliver said goodbye to the men and moseyed back up to the front of the store. It didn't take Mr. McClure long to fill the order and they were ready to leave.

"Good day Mr. McClure and fellas," said S.W and Oliver. They raised their hands in the air in a goodbye gesture to the men in the back of the store as they were finally leaving. Gilbert was pleased with his purchase. He was eating cookies before he ever got out the front door.

"Well, don't ye lads forget Election Day! Who knows what tomorrow will bring?" Mr. McClure returned to the back of the store to join the small group of men as they continued to surmise who the next President would be.

Chapter Ten
The Christmas Party, 1860

Aunt Sarah's house was a bustling place on Christmas Day. Amy Ann and Charlotte were anxiously waiting for the guests to arrive. A small pine tree decorated with very simple homemade ornaments was placed on a table in the parlor. The entranceway and steps leading to the upstairs were decorated with greenery; pine, holly, and mistletoe.

Cora was in the kitchen helping Mrs. Smith prepare the meal. Mrs. Smith had worked for Aunt Sarah for several years and she came daily to assist with the cooking and cleaning of the big house. Henry was helping in the kitchen as he often helped around the house with various chores.

Aunt Sarah placed a bowl of eggnog on the buffet table and arranged some delicate glass cups around the bowl then she very carefully mixed nutmeg, sugar, and a pint of brandy in the eggnog. Aunt Sarah's husband waited until she was gone before pouring a little more brandy and some rum into the eggnog; however, Gilbert had been watching him from a distance. Gilbert ever so quietly wandered over to inspect the beguiling concoction of spirits.

"Gilbert, my boy, have a little taste! It's good for what ails you!" Uncle Albert dipped a ladle into the bowl of eggnog and gently stirred the mix. He filled his cup to the brim. Gilbert could smell the strong liquor and nutmeg.

"No thanks, Uncle Albert. I'll try some later." Gilbert went over to sit on the piano bench and proceeded to peck on the piano keys. He attempted to play a familiar little tune that Uncle Albert recognized. Uncle Albert began singing the well-known song and swayed back and forth as he sang... *So get out de way, Ole Dan Tucker, Get out de way, Ole Dan Tucker, Get out de way, Ole Dan Tucker, You're too late to come to supper.*

Amy Ann and Charlotte heard the singing and came in the parlor to accompany Gilbert and Uncle Albert.

Amy Ann picked up the fiddle from on top of the piano and asked Gilbert if he would play the song One Horse Open Sleigh on the fiddle and she would play the piano.

"I reckon I could try it. I'm a little rusty at this," Gilbert answered. "Give me a minute to warm up."

Gilbert was the most musically inclined in the family, although the others could do a fine job of playing musical instruments as well. Aunt Sarah had given Gilbert lessons when he was growing up, although music just came naturally to him. It didn't take long for the parlor to be filled with music. Charlotte tapped on a tambourine and Uncle Albert sang along with the group.

It was apparent that Uncle Albert was enjoying himself so much so that he had another cup of eggnog after they had finished the song. He tipped the small glass cup up to his mouth and took a big drink.

"Ahh, that sure taste good! And it sure is good to be home with my family!" He sat down on the settee and got comfortable.

It was rare for Uncle Albert to be home due to his job which involved traveling around the country for the Baltimore and Ohio Railroad, exempting this special day, which he made sure he didn't miss out on. Uncle Albert was a round, plump, jovial sort of fellow and he was most jolly on this day. He had white hair with sideburns and a well-trimmed mustache and beard. His bright blue eyes had a certain mischievous look to them. He was dressed in his usual business attire; black trousers, black vest, white shirt, suspenders, and a black frock coat, except for today he wore a red cravat tied in a bow.

"Amy Ann, why don't you go to the kitchen and fetch me a little something sweet to eat? On second thought... maybe I should sneak off myself." He grinned a devilish grin and his eyes lit up as he started to get up from the settee. Aunt Sarah heard his request and ran to his side. He abruptly sat back down.

"Now... Albert, you must stay out of the kitchen. You just sit here on the settee and relax while I get you something to tide you over."

"Yes, my dear." He sat on the settee in the parlor room drinking eggnog while Aunt Sarah ran off to the kitchen. Soon she was back with a small plate of applesauce cookies which seemed satisfactory to him. Aunt Sarah had just sat down beside him when there was a knock at the door.

"My Darling, I'll get the door and you finish your cookies." Aunt Sarah affectionately patted him on the shoulder as she was getting up from the settee.

She opened the front door to find Mrs. Truby, Betsy, and Adaline carrying a basket of baked goods as a gift. Aunt Sarah graciously accepted the gift as Charlotte took their winter coats and scarves to hang up.

Samuel had dropped off Mrs. Truby, Betsy, and Adaline at the front door before going on out back to put the horse in the barn.

Amy Ann ushered them into the parlor where she encouraged everyone to admire the decorations on the tree. She cheerfully pointed out which ornaments she had made. Gilbert and Uncle Albert moved from the settee to make room for the women, only Mrs. Truby insisted on helping out in the kitchen. Aunt Sarah accompanied her to the kitchen and introduced her to Mrs. Smith.

"Cora, would you get Mrs. Truby a cup of tea and make her comfortable?" Aunt Sarah smiled and pulled out a chair from the kitchen table for Mrs. Truby.

"I'd be happy to get you a cup of tea, Mrs. Truby." Cora appeared to be in joyful spirits.

"Aunt Sarah! Someone is knocking at the door!" Amy Ann poked her head in the kitchen to summon her.

"I'm coming!" Aunt Sarah rushed to again answer the door.

She opened the door and there were S.W. and Oliver bringing in more firewood. Samuel was coming in behind them. They left their footprints in the snow. They stomped their feet on the porch to knock the snow off their boots before entering the house.

"Oh my, why thank you so much." Aunt Sarah opened the door wide to let them pass as their arms were loaded with wood. "You can take some to the parlor room and some to the kitchen."

S.W. carried the wood to the parlor where he heard Uncle Albert talking to Gilbert.

"Now, Gilbert, which one of these fine ladies is your sweetheart?" Uncle Albert was sitting by the fireplace where he packed and gently tamped tobacco in his pipe. His cup of eggnog was within easy reach on a nearby stand. Adaline heard Uncle Albert's remarks, however she thought it was said in fun to get Gilbert riled.

S.W. laid the firewood in a metal firewood rack and he observed Betsy and Adaline browsing through Aunt Sarah's collection of books that were neatly arranged in the large bookcase on the opposite side of the room.

"Miss Sarah has quite a collection of books," said Betsy to Adaline. Betsy was in awe as she inspected a few books.

"Ye is right, Betsy. I couldn't begin to read these books." Adaline addressed Betsy's observation.

Uncle Albert lit his pipe and continued to speak loudly, "Well, if I were young like you, Gilbert, I wouldn't let either of those young ladies out of my sight! It's not often you get your choice of two beautiful single young ladies!"

S.W. grinned at Gilbert as he put more wood on the fire. S.W. stood by the fire to warm up. Uncle Albert had been ogling Betsy and Adaline from across the room before he finally took notice of S.W.

"S.W., it's good to see you." Uncle Albert greeted him with a stout handshake.

S.W. remained standing in front of the fire where he had a full view of Betsy and Adaline who were still standing by the bookcase.

Uncle Albert took a slow draw on his pipe and gently blew

out smoke. He seemed to be very much enjoying the tobacco flavor. It wasn't long for the room to be filled with traces of tobacco smoke floating upward to the high ceiling while some of the smoke lingered at a lower level forming dull gray clouds.

Betsy and Adaline decided to promptly withdraw from the parlor after hearing more of Uncle Albert's comments.

"Sit down here, Gilbert!" Uncle Albert patted the seat on the chair beside him to indicate where Gilbert was to sit.

"Go over there to the pipe stand and get out a pipe and some tobacco."

Gilbert did as he was told and handed the pipe and tobacco to Uncle Albert.

"No lad, it's not for me! I'm going to teach you how to smoke a pipe!" Uncle Albert's eyes twinkled and his cheeks were a little rosy.

Gilbert was eager to learn, on the other hand, S.W. wasn't so sure it was a good idea. He cautioned Gilbert not to try smoking in the house in front of Aunt Sarah. Oliver and Samuel were listening as they were coming in the parlor to join them.

"Hmm, this should be real interesting," Oliver observed the look on Gilbert's face and smiled with amusement.

Uncle Albert jumped up from his chair. "Well, if it isn't my good men, Oliver and Samuel. Good to see you!" He gave Oliver a hearty embrace with a hard pat on the back and then gave them both a strong, firm handshake.

"Have a seat, have a seat, I say have a seat! Gilbert is about to have his first lesson on how to smoke a pipe. Hmmm, but now that you men are here... maybe... stogies are more in order." He rubbed his bearded chin and then went to the bookcase to locate a box of stogies he had hidden behind some books.

"I got these stogies in Wheeling," he said as he opened the lid on the box. "There's a big cigar factory in Wheeling. The factory has been there since 1840." Uncle Albert informed them. "Now there is a difference between a cigar and a stogie."

Uncle Albert had the gift of gab and he was well versed and articulated as he attempted to educate them on the art of smoking.

"Well...," Uncle Albert continued as he held a stogie up in the air to illustrate the difference, "a stogie is longer and thinner than a cigar." He slowly ran his fingers over the thin stogie. "It's composed of different blends of the tobacco leaf giving it a different flavor. The men on the wagon trains smoke stogies."

He was just getting ready to light the stogie when he was interrupted by very loud knocking on the front door. He placed the stogie back in the tin box and closed the lid.

"Aunt Sarah! Someone is at the door!" Amy Ann called out. Aunt Sarah didn't answer.

Uncle Albert set the box of stogies down on the table, threw his arms up in the air and shouted, "Well, for heaven's sake! Will someone get the door!" His shiny black boots made noise on the hardwood floor as he moved with haste to the front of the house. "Oh, I'll get the door myself!"

He marched out of the parlor and to the front door. Uncle Albert flung open the front door and a cold wind blew snow in the entranceway. There stood Miss Lily and the Sheriff with bags in their hands.

"Well, look what the wind blew in! If it isn't Miss Lily and the Sheriff come to visit! Come in! Come in!" Uncle Albert opened the door wider to let them pass as they carried bags in both hands.

Oliver, S.W., Gilbert, and Samuel came on the run to offer their assistance. S.W. hurriedly put on his coat and offered to take care of their horse and buggy.

"Looks like you're stayin'," said Gilbert as he took Miss Lily's bags to the top of the stairs.

Samuel helped Miss Lily with her coat and hung it up for her. The Sheriff hung his own coat on the hall tree then Uncle Albert urged the Sheriff on into the parlor to sit by the fire where he promptly offered him eggnog and a stogie.

Oliver greeted Miss Lily with a handshake. He introduced her to Amy Ann and Charlotte who were patiently waiting to meet her. Oliver slipped away to join Uncle Albert and the

Sheriff in the parlor and Amy Ann and Charlotte followed him. Samuel was now alone with Miss Lily.

"Why, Samuel, it's so good to see you again. I trust all has been well with you and your family?"

"God tis good to us," Samuel answered her. Samuel looked at her for a moment and then said, "Tis good to see that no harm has come to ye." Samuel smiled a most loving smile her way.

"Oh Samuel, I am well and no harm has come to me. Don't tell me... you were worried about me?" Miss Lily briefly maintained eye contact with him and flashed her dimpled smile. She laughed and reached out to shake his hand. It was a long handshake and Samuel could feel the warmth of her small hand as she had just removed her mittens.

Samuel remembered that dimpled smile and those snappy brown eyes. He was still astonished by her beauty and she still looked like an angel to him as she sauntered away to meet up with Aunt Sarah who had suddenly reappeared.

Uncle Albert motioned Samuel back into the parlor. Uncle Albert had discarded his pipe and he had given up on the idea of teaching Gilbert how to smoke. He was entertaining his guests with some long-winded stories about his recent travels with the railroad.

Miss Lily was standing by the table with the eggnog, enthralled by Uncle Albert's robust, storytelling voice. "Oh,

Uncle Albert, I do enjoy listening to your adventures. Do tell us more." Miss Lily encouraged him.

Gilbert brazenly spoke up, "Miss Lily, why do you speak of Uncle Albert like he's your uncle?"

Miss Lily laughed at Gilbert. "Oh, Gilbert, hasn't anyone told you? He is my uncle."

Gilbert was taken aback. "What do you mean? He is your uncle?"

"Why, Gilbert, Uncle Albert is my mother's brother." Miss Lily laughed and laughed and then helped herself to the eggnog.

Gilbert was silent for a minute before asking, "So, are we related?"

"I'm so sorry Gilbert, I would love to be related to you. You are such a handsome young man, as are your brothers. No, we aren't related, be that as it may, we share the same Uncle Albert." She placed the cup of eggnog to her lips and took a sip.

Miss Lily handed Aunt Sarah a cup of eggnog. "Here Aunt Sarah, won't you join me? It's a most delicious drink."

Aunt Sarah graciously accepted the small delicate cup of eggnog and immediately took a drink. She choked and began coughing. It took some time before she was finally able to speak.

"Albert, my dear, I think you were a bit too liberal with the spirits!" Her eyes grew wider as she was still trying to clear her throat.

"I think it tastes divine," said Miss Lily as she took another drink and sat back down on a parlor chair.

Aunt Sarah saw that Gilbert was tipping a cup of the eggnog to his lips and she promptly took it away from him.

"Really Gilbert, who gave this to you?"

Ahhh, I don't remember," Gilbert answered in haste.

The Sheriff who was standing by the piano glanced over at Aunt Sarah and smiled. He was holding a small delicate glass cup of the spirited drink in his large hand. He had placed his lit stogie in a metal ash tray on the piano.

"Sarah, my darlin', it's just a mild touch of the spirits," he spoke in his deep masculine voice. He took a drink of eggnog. "These here cups are mighty small. I think it's safe to drink." The Sheriff set the small empty cup down. He picked up his stogie from the tray and brought it to his lips.

Aunt Sarah was agitated with the Sheriff for making light of her. The Sheriff was most amused, grinned, and continued puffing on his stogie. The smoke from the stogie slowly drifted toward Aunt Sarah before floating upward to the parlor room ceiling. Aunt Sarah started on another coughing jag as she inhaled the smoke.

"I'd say it would take about a dozen of these small cups to do any harm. Come to think of it... it might do you some good to have a drink of the eggnog, Sarah." The Sheriff's tantalizing dark eyes were on Aunt Sarah as he teasingly grinned at her. "I don't need your advice Sheriff. You would do well not to worry about me." Aunt Sarah was truly irritated.

S.W. suddenly remembered the statement the Sheriff had made last summer when he and Samuel were released from jail and leaving town, "Your Aunt Sarah and I go way back." S.W. thought from the sound of their conversation that their relationship was pretty close.

Uncle Albert gave way to a quiet laugh of mild amusement and with his blue eyes twinkling he said, "Now, now, Sarah, let's not resort to any violence." Uncle Albert then suggested some musical entertainment while they waited on dinner.

Just at that exact moment Cora and Mrs. Truby came out of the kitchen to set the table. It didn't take long for the food to be brought out and everyone was called to dinner right at noon. Aunt Sarah asked S.W. to say the prayer.

The table was adorned with a large turkey placed in the middle, a huge crock filled with mashed potatoes, sausage stuffing for the turkey, biscuits, butter, jam, apple butter, cornbread, cottage cheese, and potato salad. Drinks consisted of tea, coffee, water, and of course eggnog. Dinner was followed with desserts of apple-raisin spice cake, gingerbread, applesauce, and individually prepared custard cups. Aunt Sarah served the desserts on special dessert plates. Aunt

Sarah wanted this dinner to be remembered as she thought it could well be the last time they would all be together.

After dinner, everyone gathered in the parlor to relax and open their presents that were under the small tree. Amy Ann was the most excited with her paper dolls from New York that Uncle Albert had brought back for her. Later when the presents were opened, the conversation became lively with the Sheriff, Uncle Albert, and Miss Lily telling stories with much merriment which kept everyone entertained.

S.W. and Adaline hoped they could spend some quiet time together in the kitchen since Mrs. Smith had gone home and Henry had retreated to his small shack in the woods at the back of the property. S.W. and Adaline were shocked when they opened the kitchen door to find Cora lying on the floor doubled over in pain and barely able to speak.

"Hurry, Adaline, get Aunt Sarah!" S.W. took immediate action. He knelt on the floor to check her breathing and put his arms around Cora to hold her in an upright position until Aunt Sarah got there.

Adaline went screaming for Aunt Sarah. Aunt Sarah rushed into the kitchen closely followed by Amy Ann, Charlotte, and Gilbert. The Sheriff recognized the need to keep the others back until the situation was under control and for everyone to stay calm.

"Cora! Cora! What is wrong?" Aunt Sarah was gripping

Cora's hand, but Cora's eyes were tightly closed and she didn't answer. Cora's hands felt cold and clammy.

"Quickly, carry her upstairs to bed!" Aunt Sarah ordered S.W. and she ordered everyone else to get back and give them room to get by.

"Aunt Sarah!" Amy Ann screamed, "Is she going to be alright?"

Gilbert barged ahead of S.W. to open the bedroom door and to pull back the covers on the bed.

"Gilbert, run as fast as you can and get the doctor!" S.W. said as he placed Cora on the bed.

"Yes!" Gilbert grabbed his coat and was out the door in a flash.

Aunt Sarah sent orders for someone to bring warm water and clean washing clothes to the room then she ordered everyone else out except for Mrs. Truby.

"Cora! Cora, please speak to me! Open your eyes!" Aunt Sarah called out with a look of panic on her face.

"Cora tis with child!" said Mrs. Truby. "Tis time for baby to come?"

Cora moaned and kept her eyes closed. "No, No, it's not time." Cora managed to faintly speak.

Aunt Sarah was not prepared for this event and she worried about how she would explain this. Only she knew the truth about Cora and now her plan to hide the truth was shattered. Would they believe that Mrs. Johnson's nephew had forced himself on Cora? Maybe they would accuse Cora of enticing the nephew? Aunt Sarah tried hard to think of what would be best for Cora and the baby. She wanted to say that Cora's husband was of no account and had run off when he was told that Cora was carrying a child. What Aunt Sarah really wanted was for Cora and the baby to stay with her so that she could finally have a baby in the house to hold and to keep for herself.

"Cora, ye need to get undressed and put on a nightgown before the doctor gets here." Mrs. Truby was taking charge of the situation.

Cora moaned again and tried to sit at the edge of the bed, only she was entirely too weak to hold herself up. Aunt Sarah came to her senses and began helping. Charlotte came with warm water and clean towels, sheets and bathing clothes. They could hear the commotion downstairs when the doctor arrived. There was loud talking in the entranceway when Gilbert and the doctor entered.

"Here, I'll hang up your coat, Doc! She's right up there!" Gilbert pointed up the stairs. "Can I come too?" Gilbert asked.

"No, son, you better stay down here. I'll let you know if I need you." The doctor's voice was calm and reassuring.

Everyone gathered in the parlor to wait for news of Cora's condition. S.W. put more wood on the fire in the parlor and

Oliver took care of the stove in the kitchen. Gilbert and S.W. paced the floor worrying about Cora as they suddenly realized how fond they were of her. Others could be heard speculating about what could be the matter with Cora. Betsy and Adaline decided this would be a good time to serve coffee and hot tea with cookies and cake so they went to the kitchen to prepare a tray. Miss Lily asked if she could join them in the kitchen to help. Once they were in the kitchen, Adaline and Betsy told Miss Lily that they had been praying for the Lord to keep Cora safe and make her well.

"Yes, may the Lord keep her in his care. Thank you both for praying. I know Gilbert is terribly upset by the way he has been pacing the floor. He just can't sit still. And S.W. has certainly been a big help," Miss Lily observed.

"We have all grown fond of Cora," Adaline spoke as she helped prepare the tray of food. "Gilbert is a tender-hearted lad, more than ye might think him to be."

Only now did S.W. come to realize what was amiss about Cora, but he dared not speculate to the others.

The clock on the fireplace mantel ticked away the time until an hour had passed. The clock chimed and all conversation ceased. The silence was interrupted by the sound of footsteps coming down the stairs. The Doctor entered the parlor and motioned for Uncle Albert to come closer so they could discuss in private the details of what just happened. Uncle Albert suggested they go in the kitchen and the Doctor agreed. Uncle Albert asked Adaline, Betsy, and Miss Lily to please leave the kitchen for a moment.

"Why, certainly, Uncle Albert, we understand." Miss Lily held the door open for Adaline to carry the tray.

The Doctor didn't waste any time explaining what had happened. "The young woman, Cora, was with child. I believe the child to have been full term. I regret that I wasn't able to save the baby, however the young woman will be alright. She needs all the bedrest she can get. She is very weak." Doctor paused then continued with instructions. "You need to contact the undertaker right away. The sooner the better for the sake of the young woman."

"Oh, my, I don't know what to say." Uncle Albert sat down at the table and offered the Doctor a seat as well. "This is shocking news. I wasn't expecting this. I knew nothing about this. I suppose Sarah knew of it?"

"Yes," said the Doctor. "Sarah knew all about it and she had hoped to keep the young woman and child here. I know how Sarah goes about trying to help everyone." The Doctor judged from the look on Uncle Albert's face that he needed a little direction. "Now, Albert, I'll send S.W. over to get the undertaker. Would you like for me to break the news to your guests and send them all home?"

"What? What's that you say?" Uncle Albert was dazed.

"Never mind, Albert. You just sit here and let it all soak in. I'll take care of it for you."

The Doctor went directly to S.W. and sent him to the undertaker's, then he explained things to the Sheriff so the Sheriff could get things under control. The Doctor knew the Sheriff would handle the situation gently.

The Sheriff announced the tragedy and proceeded to tell everyone that they could stay and help Miss Sarah or go home.

"Now, I know you are all good folks and kind hearted people, nevertheless, we don't know all the details that surround this situation. So, it would be a kindness and the Christian thing to do... not to spread rumors! Am I clear on that?" The Sheriff sounded more demanding than questioning.

"Yes, sir," replied Betsy and Adaline. Everyone else nodded in agreement except for Gilbert.

Gilbert was angry. He was angry at the man who was responsible for causing all this pain and hurting Cora. He sensed it was Mrs. Johnson's nephew. "This must have happened in Cincinnati!" Gilbert said out loud as he ran up the stairs to Cora's room. Gilbert flung open the door, but when he entered the room he simmered down. He saw Aunt Sarah holding the lifeless little bundle in her lap. She sat in a chair beside the bed where Cora lie. Mrs. Truby left the room to go after more warm water and soap to clean with. She carried a basket of bloody bedclothes downstairs.

"Come over here, Gilbert," Cora whispered. "Take a look at my little darling."

Gilbert didn't want to look at the baby.

Aunt Sarah pulled back the blanket so Gilbert could see his fat baby face. Tears streamed down Aunt Sarah's cheeks.

Cora looked at Gilbert with pleading eyes and said, "I'm sorry, Gilbert. I didn't tell you the truth. You remember that day I told you about living in Cincinnati and Mrs. Johnson's nephew?"

"Yeah, I know!" Gilbert yelled at her. "I thought you were my friend and you trusted me! Why didn't you trust enough to tell me about Mrs. Johnson's nephew? He forced himself on you... didn't he?"

Gilbert ran out of the room and down the stairs where he grabbed his coat and hat from the hall tree and ran outside. He ran to Henry's shack in the woods to take solace in being alone with Henry. "Henry would understand and help sort this out." The thoughts rushed through Gilbert's mind as he ran through the yard with the cold air hitting against his face.

Mrs. Truby asked Adaline and Betsy to help clean up the kitchen and she explained that they would be going home as soon as the undertaker arrived. Samuel heard the conversation and he agreed it would be best to leave as soon as possible to give the family time alone.

Uncle Albert, Oliver, and the Sheriff were in the parlor.

The Sheriff was attempting to console Uncle Albert. Uncle Albert thought he had been betrayed by Aunt Sarah. Uncle Albert took a swig of brandy straight from the bottle and plopped down on the settee.

"You fellows want a drink?" He held the bottle up in the air and waved it around.

"No, no thanks, Uncle Albert," answered Oliver.

"My Darling Sarah has schemed and plotted behind my back! I ask you, what kind of woman would do that?" Uncle Albert took another drink.

Miss Lily entered the parlor just as Uncle Albert was asking the question.

"A very kind and caring woman and that's the kind of woman Aunt Sarah is. You know that, Uncle Albert. Now, let's proceed with making the necessary arrangements before the undertaker gets here." Miss Lily sat across from Uncle Albert looking directly at him.

"I just can't do it. You do it Lily. You're good at this sort of thing," Uncle Albert requested.

"Very well, I'll go now before the undertaker gets here," Miss Lily stood up, straightened her dress and mentally prepared herself for the unpleasant task.

Samuel placed his hand on Miss Lily's shoulder as she passed by him. She paused momentarily before going up the stairs.

"Lily, ye is a strong woman, but ye will remember to be gentle to a young grieving mother and to Aunt Sarah."

"Of course, Samuel." Miss Lily said as she climbed the steps.

"Can we go too? Please, may we go?" Amy Ann begged as Charlotte followed her up the steps.

Miss Lily looked at Samuel for his approval and he nodded his head. They gathered in the bedroom and tried to come to terms with what had happened.

"Cora," Miss Lily said, "do you have clothes for the baby?"

Cora spoke very faintly as a tear flowed down her cheek.

"Baby clothes are in the dresser." She pointed to the dresser next to the bed. "Miss Sarah and I have made lots of clothes. We would stay up late into the night making clothes."

"Have you thought about a name? You will want a name on the marker, won't you?" Miss Lily kindly said.

"Oh... I need a little time to think on that," Cora replied.

"Well, certainly you can take your time. Maybe Aunt Sarah has some ideas? Charlotte and Amy Ann could help with names." Miss Lily sat down on a chair near the fireplace in the bedroom.

Surprisingly Aunt Sarah spoke up, "I must send for the preacher!" She handed the small lifeless bundle to Cora and ran down the stairs shouting that someone must go immediately and get the preacher.

Oliver was the first to console Aunt Sarah. Oliver offered to find the preacher and bring him back to the house immediately.

Just then there was a loud knock at the front door and Uncle Albert could be heard talking with the undertaker. Cora had a hard time letting go of her precious little boy. S.W. gently carried the baby downstairs to the undertaker and Miss Lily followed him.

"Oh, and one more thing," added Miss Lily, "the name on the marker is to be Baby Gilbert Johnson."

Chapter Eleven
January 1861

Christmas at Aunt Sarah's was one they would not forget. Cora was better now following plenty of bedrest, still she was having a hard time coming to grips with the loss of her child. Those who had gathered on Christmas Day at Aunt Sarah's came to the small service at the church for the baby's burial. It was a cold winter day when Gilbert and S.W. carried the small casket to the gravesite.

Miss Lily had stayed over longer than she had originally planned to help at the house and keep Amy Ann and Charlotte occupied as well as to comfort Cora and Aunt Sarah. Miss Lily was surprised to learn that Aunt Sarah had been looking forward to having a baby in the house as Aunt Sarah had never mentioned longing for a child.

A letter arrived in late January regarding Mrs. Johnson's estate. Aunt Sarah was concerned that the investigation wasn't moving along fast enough, so she had contacted her lawyer again. Aunt Sarah casually laid the letter on the kitchen table. Unbeknownst to her, Gilbert took the liberty of reading it. This was big news to Gilbert of which he didn't take lightly. Gilbert began to make plans to take matters into his own hands. Gilbert was determined to learn more about Mrs. Johnson's nephew and even more determined to visit Cincinnati. Gilbert quickly put the letter back on the kitchen table before Aunt Sarah noticed him reading it.

"Gilbert, would you mind going to the store for me?"

"Sure, Aunt Sarah, I'll go." Gilbert was looking very innocent.

"It won't take me, but a minute or two to make a list."

Mrs. Smith was in the kitchen cooking and Aunt Sarah was still sitting at the table with Gilbert when Henry came in the backdoor with an armful of firewood. Gilbert sat patiently waiting. Henry was whistling a happy tune as he stacked the wood on the floor.

"Why, Henry, what makes you so happy?" Aunt Sarah asked.

"Why, Miss Sarah, there ain't no call to be sad all the time. Ya just gotta take one day at a time and be thankful." Henry was smiling as he stood up from stacking the wood on the floor.

Cora came in the kitchen and heard Henry's remark. "You

are so right, Henry. I have a lot to be thankful for. I'm thankful for everyone here in this kitchen." Cora hugged Aunt Sarah and Gilbert, then she put her arms around Henry's shoulders. "Mrs. Smith, if you weren't so busy cooking, I'd hug you too."

"Cora, poor girl, it's good to see you up and about," Mrs. Smith said as she stood at the stove stirring the stew in the big kettle. "You know you really need to take it easy dear and get your health back."

"Thank you, Mrs. Smith. I need to be with people. I'm lonely."

"I know you are, dear girl, things will get better," Mrs. Smith said, gently trying to soothe the pain that Cora felt.

Cora sat down at the table as Aunt Sarah finished printing the list of items and handed it to Gilbert.

"Gilbert, here is the list. Henry can go with you and help you carry the supplies home."

Gilbert put the list in his coat pocket and pulled his hat down over his ears. Henry stood by the door waiting. Aunt Sarah poured Cora a cup of tea and sat down with her as Gilbert and Henry were leaving.

It didn't take long for Gilbert and Henry to get to Mr. McClure's General Store. A couple of customers were standing in the back of the store huddled up next to the stove. Gilbert didn't recognize the men and he thought they might just be passing through. Mr. McClure stopped talking with them and came up front to wait on Gilbert.

"What can I do for ye, Gilbert?" Mr. McClure spoke loudly.

"Oh, Aunt Sarah needs a few things for the house." Gilbert handed Mr. McClure the list from his coat pocket and Henry waited by the door.

Mr. McClure took the list and went behind the counter to begin packing the items.

"I'm right sorry 'bout what happened over at Miss Sarah's on Christmas Day." Mr. McClure sounded sincere. He placed a bag of sugar on the counter and turned back around to get a container of cinnamon off the shelf.

Gilbert's face turned red as the statement made him very angry.

"Folks in this town talk too much, 'specially 'bout things they know nothin' 'bout!" Gilbert blurted out.

Mr. McClure turned around to face Gilbert and replied, "Now lad, there ain't no call to get upset. A lot of folks come in this store and they're good people. Most folks are just concerned and want to express their sorrow for ye family. Lad, ye need to remember that other folks has lost loved ones too."

Gilbert settled down after hearing what Mr. McClure had to say. "Ahhh, I reckon you're right, Mr. McClure. It was just such a blow to all of us. We ain't got over it yet."

The two men in the back of the store came up front to stand by the counter. One of the men had a mug of coffee in his hand and the other man was smoking a pipe. The man with the pipe looked out of place standing in Mr. McClure's store as he was dressed in nice looking business apparel. Gilbert surveyed the two and he wondered what business they had in town. Gilbert was just about to ask them their names and where they came from when the gentleman with the pipe spoke up.

"Nice to meet you Gilbert." The man with the pipe reached out his hand to Gilbert. "My name is Mr. Hayes. I'm a lawyer from Cincinnati," he stated. Gilbert was reluctant to shake his hand. It took Gilbert a moment to assess the man and accept his out-stretched hand.

The man continued to explain why he was in town. "I believe it is your Aunt Sarah that I'm looking for. Would you be so kind as to direct us to her home when you are finished here?" The tall man with a dark complexion leaned against the counter with his pipe in hand, waiting for Gilbert to reply.

"Well, sir, I don't rightly know if that would be the right thing to do." Gilbert paused to think for a second and then said, "Seein' how I don't know you or what your business is. Could be that Aunt Sarah don't want any visitors."

"Well, Gilbert, I can assure you that she wants to see me," said the man. Gilbert could smell the smoke from the man's pipe. Gilbert thought the tobacco was of a better quality than most folks smoked in this part of the country.

Mr. McClure was still working on filling the order, however he was intently listening to the conversation between Gilbert and the man with the pipe, Mr. Hayes.

"Seems to me that a gentleman would have sent a message ahead of time to announce his arrival." Gilbert was adamant.

"It's good to see you are an observant young lad. How do you know I didn't send word?" Mr. Hayes questioned Gilbert.

"Well, Aunt Sarah did get a letter, anyhow I don't recall anythin' 'bout you comin' to visit," said Gilbert.

Mr. McClure was almost finished packing the wooden crate and bagging the small items when he turned to Gilbert.

"Gilbert, of course this is none of my business, but ye could send Henry on ahead to get Miss Sarah's approval."

"Certainly," said Mr. Hayes. "Then when Henry comes back we can get down to business." Mr. Hayes looked very pleased with the solution.

"Go ahead Henry and be sure to tell Aunt Sarah the man's name is Hayes, a lawyer from Cincinnati. We'll just wait right here for you to return with Aunt Sarah's answer."

The two men returned to the back of the store to sit by the fire and drink coffee while Gilbert remained in the front of the store waiting for Henry.

When Henry came back he was driving Aunt Sarah's enclosed buggy with Aunt Sarah in it. Henry tied the horse and buggy to the hitching post and helped Aunt Sarah down. Aunt

Sarah looked disheveled with her hair and clothing in disarray from hurrying to get to Mr. McClure's General Store and the wind had blown her bonnet off her head on the way over. Henry helped her up the porch steps and into the store while Gilbert held the front door open as she entered.

"Gilbert, what is all this commotion?" Aunt Sarah demanded to know.

Gilbert was dumbfounded when he saw Aunt Sarah with her hair a mess and her bonnet sitting cockeyed on her head. He couldn't speak for thinking about how ridiculous she looked. Mr. McClure quickly guided her to the back of the store where he hurried to get her a chair by the stove where the two men were waiting. He introduced her to Mr. Hayes and to the other man who was the driver for Mr. Hayes.

"Well, I dare say, Mr. Hayes, I did not receive a formal announcement or even a telegram regarding your arrival! This is most inconvenient, meeting you here in the General Store!" Aunt Sarah was extremely perturbed with Mr. Hayes.

"Please excuse me, for all that, I can assure you that a letter expressing my intent to meet with you was sent and you should have received it a few days ago. At any rate, there have been new developments of great interest in the matter concerning Mrs. Johnson's estate and her nephew. I thought it would be better to discuss this in the privacy of your home rather than ask you to travel all the way to Cincinnati in this weather." Mr. Hayes was clearly disturbed by Aunt Sarah's rude behavior.

Aunt Sarah's demeanor instantly changed when she learned of new developments. "Well... now... Mr. Hayes, this is good news?" Aunt Sarah raised her eyebrows in question.

"I suggest we go immediately to your home to speak in private?" Mr. Hayes calmly requested.

"Certainly, please follow my carriage." Aunt Sarah replied and promptly went to the front of the store and waited for Mr. Hayes to put on his coat and hat.

"Gilbert, would you be so kind as to load these items into the buggy?" Aunt Sarah said as she pointed to the wooden crate sitting on the counter.

It was hard for Gilbert to contain his laughter as he once again looked at her cockeyed bonnet. He picked up the crate and went out the door as she stopped to thank Mr. McClure.

Once Aunt Sarah was back in her home, she saw her reflection in the mirror and immediately straightened her hair before Mr. Hayes arrived. Miss Lily hurried down the stairway when she heard Aunt Sarah coming in the house.

"Aunt Sarah, why have you been out this early in the morning? Is something the matter?" Miss Lily looked worried.

"Oh, my dear, I can't explain it now. I have company arriving soon, very soon!" Aunt Sarah was clearly in a rush to make herself look presentable as she continued to smooth her hair into place.

Gilbert barged through the kitchen door to meet with Aunt Sarah. "Aunt Sarah, I'm goin' to help the driver for Mr. Hayes put his horse in the barn and I'll tell him to wait in the kitchen with Henry." Gilbert quickly added, "Don't you think I should stay for this meetin' with Mr. Hayes?"

"Gilbert, the only thing you need to do is to put more wood on the fire in the parlor and keep still!" Aunt Sarah was visibly jittery. She wrung her hands and smoothed down her hair some more. "Oh, very well, Gilbert, go and help the driver."

Miss Lily attempted to calm Aunt Sarah when she noticed how jittery she was. "Why, Aunt Sarah, you are positively uneasy about something. Please come sit and allow me to get you a drink of brandy to calm your nerves." Miss Lily guided her by the arm into the parlor to sit by the fire as Aunt Sarah seemed to be in a daze.

Just as Aunt Sarah was seated, there was a loud rap at the front door and Miss Lily hurried to answer it with Gilbert following hot on her heels. A blast of cold air swept through as the door was opened and the tall man with a dark complexion stood in the doorway.

"How do you do, Ma'am? I'm looking for..."

"I know who you're lookin' for. Aunt Sarah is right in there." Gilbert boldly interrupted the man and pointed to the parlor room where Aunt Sarah was sitting.

Miss Lily gave Gilbert a very disapproving look before telling the man to come in.

"I am Mr. Hayes." He offered his hand to her and she accepted his handshake.

"It's very nice to meet you, Mr. Hayes. I am Miss Lily Baramore."

"It's very nice to meet you, Miss Baramore." Mr. Hayes removed his hat and Miss Lily placed it on top of the coat rack.

"May I take your coat?" Miss Lily gestured to him with open arms.

"Yes, thank you," said Mr. Hayes as he removed his coat, gloves and hat.

Finally, Aunt Sarah was able to compose herself and got up to welcome Mr. Hayes into her home. She explained to Miss Lily that Mr. Hayes was the lawyer who was investigating Mrs. Johnson's estate settlement.

After learning the nature of his visit Miss Lily charmingly escorted him to the parlor and poured him a drink of brandy. She engaged him in casual conversation about Cincinnati. He was impressed with her knowledge of the city as well as her theatrical accomplishments.

Gilbert was getting annoyed with the conversation as he sat on the settee rapidly tapping his foot on the floor.

"Really Gilbert, must you continually tap your foot on the floor?" Aunt Sarah sat beside him and spoke in a low tone.

"Well, why can't we just get to the point?" Gilbert leaned near her and whispered.

Aunt Sarah looked very stern and replied, "Gilbert, would you please go to the kitchen and have Mrs. Smith prepare a pot of tea and a tray of cookies and cake for our company?"

Reluctantly, Gilbert acted on Aunt Sarah's request.

While Gilbert was gone, Mr. Hayes did get to the point and he began by stating that Mr. Johnson had been under surveillance due to reports that he was a Southern sympathizer and was an active member of the KGC.

"Mr. Hayes, this is most interesting, whatever is the KGC?" Miss Lily wanted to know.

Aunt Sarah sat on the settee and listened quietly trying to make sense of it all.

Mr. Hayes explained, "The KGC is also known as the Knights of the Golden Circle. They are a pro-slavery secret society that propose a separate confederation of slave states to increase the power of the Southern slave holders. The KGC headquarters are in Cincinnati. Mr. Johnson could be imprisoned for his activities with the KGC."

Miss Lily poured more brandy in the glass that Mr. Hayes was holding and then she asked, "I don't understand what this has to do with Mrs. Johnson's estate?"

Mr. Hayes held the glass to his lips and took a sip of the brandy. "The court won't look favorably on Mr. Johnson if we can prove he is a member of the KGC. Furthermore, we can now present the will that Mrs. Johnson had prepared. It was discovered in a small locked trunk at the bank and the document was just recently released into my care and keeping."

"You have discovered a will that Mrs. Johnson had prepared?" Aunt Sarah looked at Mr. Hayes with wide-eyed wonder.

Mr. Hayes took a seat on the settee beside Aunt Sarah and pulled out the folded document from the inside of his dress coat pocket. He handed the document to Aunt Sarah and further explained, "This document along with other valuables and money were found in a small locked trunk stored in the attic at the bank."

Aunt Sarah was stunned to learn that Mrs. Johnson had bequeathed all of her property and possessions to Cora. In the will, Mrs. Johnson had praised Cora for being a faithful and hardworking servant and caretaker.

Gilbert had been listening as he stood in the doorway of the parlor. As soon as he heard the news, he ran to the kitchen to inform Cora. Gilbert threw open the door to the kitchen and yelled, "Good news, Cora! Come into the parlor and meet Mr. Hayes. Hurry, hurry, come fast!" Gilbert was wild with excitement.

"Gilbert, what are you talking about?" Cora was very

confused.

Gilbert grabbed hold of her arm and pulled her through the kitchen doorway and on through into the parlor to join the others. "Mr. Hayes, this is Cora! Tell her the news!" Gilbert demanded.

Aunt Sarah stood up and instructed Cora to join them. She motioned for Cora to come sit with her on the settee as she introduced Mr. Hayes.

"Cora, Mr. Hayes has discovered some very important information and he traveled all the way here from Cincinnati to inform us. I think you will be most pleased," Aunt Sarah smiled at Cora.

Miss Lily excused herself and went to the kitchen to help prepare the refreshment tray and hot tea.

Mr. Hayes quickly explained the Will to Cora and added that a court date would be set for a hearing. Lastly he added, "This could take some time."

"I don't know what to say." Cora was having a hard time accepting the realization that Mrs. Johnson had bequeathed her everything. Cora sat silently in thought for a few moments.

"I know what to say," Gilbert rushed into the conversation. "That scoundrel nephew of Mrs. Johnson's doesn't deserve a thing. Cora, you deserve to have the place 'specially after what that scoundrel did to you!"

Mr. Hayes looked interested, raising his dark eyebrows at

Cora. "Is there something more I should know?"

Cora was in tears and unable to speak so Aunt Sarah explained everything in short detail to Mr. Hayes. Mr. Hayes took mental notes which he planned to record later in his legal journal. Mr. Hayes stood up, walked over to Cora and took hold of her hand.

"My deepest apologies to you. I regret that this tragedy happened, in spite of all this, I am pleased to tell you that just a little while longer and you will be recompensed." Mr. Hayes let go of Cora's hand and put the document back in the inside pocket of his dress coat.

Miss Lily entered and called everyone into the dining room for refreshments. When Aunt Sarah came to the table Miss Lily handed her a letter.

"Oh, Aunt Sarah, I found a page from your letter on the kitchen floor under the table. I hope it wasn't anything important?" Miss Lily looked puzzled.

"Thank you, Lily," Aunt Sarah said as she took a look at the letter.

"Oh my goodness, this is the notification of your arrival, Mr. Hayes. I must have dropped it on the floor earlier this morning. Mr. Hayes, please accept my apology."

Gilbert knew he was the one responsible for dropping it on the floor. He definitely was not going to admit to that.

"An apology is not needed. All is well and it is nice to be in the company of such lovely ladies." Mr. Hayes was particularly looking at Miss Lily when he made the statement.

Gilbert loudly cleared his throat when he noticed Mr. Hayes staring at Miss Lily. Gilbert spoon sugared his hot tea and vigorously stirred it before taking a drink. He had a big bite of cake ready to put in his mouth when he decided to ask Cora some questions.

"Cora, what do you plan on doin' with the big house? Maybe you could open up a shop of some kind or you could take in boarders?" Gilbert sounded enthusiastic. He shoved a big bite of cake in his mouth and asked Aunt Sarah to pass him the pitcher of milk which he poured into a large mug and quickly gulped down.

"Really Gilbert, it's too soon to be asking Cora such questions. Now finish your cake and when you're finished, you can go upstairs and tell Charlotte and Amy Ann to come down and meet Mr. Hayes." Aunt Sarah took a sip of hot tea.

"Ahhh, alright, I'll go now." Gilbert scooted his chair out from the table and ran up the stairs.

"Mr. Hayes, will you be staying the night?" Miss Lily asked.

"I would like to get some rest before going back. Is there a hotel or boardinghouse in town?" Mr. Hayes questioned.

Aunt Sarah was quick to cordially invite Mr. Hayes to be a guest in her home. "Mr. Hayes, we have an extra room. You are more than welcome to stay here. Your driver could sleep in the room with Gilbert."

"Why, thank you, Ma'am. That is most hospitable of you," said Mr. Hayes. "Please excuse me while I advise my driver of the arrangements."

Miss Lily showed him to the kitchen where the driver was waiting and was just finishing the nice warm meal that Mrs. Smith had prepared for him. Mr. Hayes explained the overnight sleeping arrangements to the driver and they settled in for the evening.

The next day after the departure of Mr. Hayes, there was a lot of speculation amongst the family and Cora concerning the recent news that Mr. Hayes had delivered. Everyone seemed to have their own ideas on what would be best for Cora to do with the grand house, including Miss Lily, who was formulating plans that would benefit herself as well as Cora.

"Well, Cora, I really do think I could help you turn your home into a profitable business since I do have many friends in Cincinnati who would be more than helpful in getting the word out and around to draw in customers." Miss Lily was noticeably excited about her plan.

"What kind of profitable business do you have in mind, Miss Lily?" Cora skeptically questioned.

"Well, Cora, I well know what a fine cook you are and with my acquaintances in the theater, you could open a boardinghouse and have your pick of the most influential guests." Miss Lily's dark brown eyes shined like stars as she spoke.

"I must admit, Miss Lily, you are very encouraging, however, it seems to me that wealthy folks would expect fancy food and drinks. I know I would fail at such an endeavor as I am only a lowly servant," Cora replied as she felt discouraged.

"Cora! You must not put yourself down! You are a beautiful and intelligent woman!" Miss Lily blurted forth the words as she quickly rose from her chair. "You can do anything you set your mind to do and I will help you!" Miss Lily declared.

"Yes, Cora, you can do anything you want with that big house! And you are beautiful and smart!" Gilbert boldly announced. He was as determined as Miss Lily to give Cora a much needed push.

"Well, Cora, you have plenty of time to think on it. There is no hurry. Let not this blessing become an irritation," Aunt Sarah said, putting an end to the discussion.

The winter months went by and nothing more was said or heard about concerning Mrs. Johnson's estate or her nephew. Aunt Sarah decided it was time to send another letter to the Lawyer Hayes and so more time went by as they waited on news from Cincinnati.

Chapter Twelve
Spring 1861

❧

A few of Mr. McClure's regular customers stood around the old wood burning stove in the back of McClure's General Store on this chilly spring morning. Mr. McClure looked worried as they discussed their concerns about the war.

"I reckon the whole country is in a state of upheaval. Ye know that six states have already seceded from the Union! The country is split, I tell ye split, North and South. I don't know where this is all goin'. It is a mighty sorry state of affairs," Mr. McClure voiced his opinion.

"Well, what do ya reckon Lincoln will do about it?" Old Dan Sellers asked Mr. McClure.

"I can't say, except I reckon we're headed for hard times. A good many of our lads will go off and enlist." Mr. McClure rubbed his chin as he sat down on an old battered chair to relax and exchange views with the others.

Old Dan readily reported, "The Donaldsons have a few

boys. They might consider joining up and there are plenty of other lads around here in their twenties. Might be some of our married men will go off too?"

Samuel came through the front door just as Old Dan continued to speculate on who would join up and who wouldn't. Samuel walked to the back of the store to get warmed by the fire and joined in the conversation.

"Well, who will plow the fields and take care of the women and children if all the young men go off and enlist?" Samuel inquired.

The undertaker stood up from his seat and buttoned up his coat as he was getting ready to leave. "I've heard all I want to hear. We sit here far removed from what is really taking place in our country. Our little town will soon be filled with sorrow when our young boys don't come home. Might not be all young men, could be some of the others will enlist."

Samuel was angry. "That's a heartless thing to say!"

The undertaker looked at the other men and then looked at Samuel and said, "Samuel, it's just the cold reality of which I speak." The undertaker then put on his hat.

"Good day to you gentlemen." The undertaker tipped his hat to them and wasted no time leaving.

"He's right ya know...," Old Dan pondered on what the undertaker had to say.

Mr. McClure could hear the bitterness in Samuel's voice

so before Samuel had a chance to expand on his thoughts Mr. McClure asked, "Well, Samuel, what will ye be needin' today?"

"Oh, I better stock up on sugar and coffee since some folks say it could soon be hard to come by." Samuel spoke sarcastically as he followed Mr. McClure to the front counter to fill his order.

The month of March proved to be worrisome for most folks in the county, especially families with young men, as they continued with plans to plow their fields and plant crops.

All the recent hoopla made Gilbert just as rambunctious as ever and he spent a lot of time at the Donaldsons' place listening in on their discussions and the newest reports coming in by way of letters and the newspapers.

It was April 17th, 1861, when Gilbert came running into the house after spending the afternoon over at the Donaldsons' place. He was anxiously explaining the latest news to Charlotte and Amy Ann.

"Mr. Donaldson says the war has started. The Confederates opened fire on Fort Sumter and Lincoln is callin' for 75,000 militiamen volunteers!" Gilbert was talking fast and out of breath.

"Now, Gilbert, just slow down and take it easy," said Charlotte. "There's no reason for you to get so all fired up."

S.W. and Oliver were just coming in from feeding the livestock. There was still a chill in the air even though it was springtime. They took off their muddy boots and placed them in front of the open flames of the fireplace to dry.

"Well, Gilbert, what makes you so excited?" Oliver asked as he stood in front of the fire to get warm.

"I was just over at the Donaldsons' and their Pa says the war has started! The Confederates opened fire on Fort Sumter and now Lincoln is callin' for 75,000 militiamen!" Gilbert impatiently moved about the kitchen as he located the crock of cookies. He removed the lid and took out a handful of gingersnaps.

Oliver calmly responded, "Well, I reckon there's no reason for us to worry. Kentucky is still neutral so maybe the fighting won't cross the Ohio River."

S.W. was thinking about what Mr. McClure had said to him last summer, "There might come a day when ye need some weapons on that farm." S.W. still didn't want to think of enlisting in the Union Army, although he thought he might be making that decision very soon.

Amy Ann was very solemn as she helped Charlotte prepare the table for the evening meal. "All this talk of war makes me gloomy. I don't like it! I hope the war never comes this way."

In an effort to cheer Amy Ann, S.W. pulled his harmonica from off the top of the fireplace mantel and blew into it.

"This old thing still works! After we eat we can have a little music."

"Good," said Gilbert, "I'll get out the fiddle."

"Yes indeed, that's just what we need!" Charlotte exclaimed. "And when the roads dry up from all this rain we can plan a gathering at Aunt Sarah's house?" Charlotte tried to build up happy times for Amy Ann.

"That would be grand!" Amy Ann excitedly threw her hands up in the air and danced around the kitchen.

"Sure... Aunt Sarah loves to have company!" Gilbert was all for any gathering where there was food.

The war continued growing over the spring and summer months, without regard to all the talk, life in Perry Township was unchanged as most folks thought the war would end soon. However, as time went on; reports of suffering on the battlefields and skirmishes continued to be in the newspapers. Rumors circulated with some local folks receiving letters from friends and relatives who lived near the fighting and witnessed the war. Concern increased as the war progressed and people passing through the area gave actual accounts of the battlefields and wounded soldiers.

By Sunday, August 18th, S.W. and Samuel were seriously considering enlisting in the Union Army, but it wasn't until the preacher gave his sermon that they made their decision.

Charlotte, Amy Ann, Oliver, S.W. and Gilbert, along with lots of other folks including the Truby family, gathered at the church on Sunday to listen to the preacher give a report about the war. He had recently traveled to Washington D.C. and saw firsthand some of the casualties of the war. He emphasized the need for supplies and help in the field hospitals and he reported seeing women working in the field hospitals as nurses as well as other women doing laundry, cooking, and doing whatever was needed.

In conclusion, the preacher stood in the front of the congregation and made a request. "And so... my friends... as workers for the Lord," he paused to point a finger at the crowd. "You can help these brave men and women! Won't you join me in gathering and organizing supplies for the hospitals? Now, let us pray for much needed guidance."

After the service, many stayed to discuss what was needed and how they could be of help.

S.W. and Adaline met outside the church before going home. They were equally concerned, not only about the war, but about their future together. After hearing what they considered to be an accurate report, they were even more worried.

"Oh, S.W., I don't know what I shall do if ye leave me? I shan't bear it." Adaline and S.W. stood beside the buggy hidden from view.

S.W. held Adaline close to him, pressing her petite body against him, with his strong arms surrounding her. S.W.

looked around to make sure no one was coming before he spoke.

"Adaline, you know I love you." He kissed her on the forehead and then on the lips before he helped her into the buggy. "You know I've always loved you. You're the one for me. We better talk about this later." S.W. briefly held her hand before Betsy swiftly came around the buggy.

"S.W., tis good to see ye in church today." Betsy smiled with a curious look in her eyes as if to question his intent. Her brown eyes seemed to pry into his very thoughts.

"Good to see you, Betsy. Here, allow me to help you up," S.W. politely offered.

"Thank ye." Betsy held out her arm so he could steady her as she climbed onto the buggy seat. Once Betsy was seated she asked, "Well, I wonder what is keepin' Samuel and Mama so long?"

"I reckon they're still talking to the preacher since he had so much to report and he did say the field hospitals were in need of supplies," S.W. reasoned. "Maybe they want to offer their help."

"Well, we can barely keep the farm goin' as it is with only Samuel workin' the fields. How can folks like us, be expected to help? I hope Samuel isn't thinkin' 'bout runnin' off to fight in the war?" Betsy's voice was filled with despair.

"Really, Betsy, calm down," said Adaline. "Ye know the

preacher didn't say a thing 'bout runnin' off to fight. He merely spoke of helpin' the wounded soldiers in the field hospitals. Samuel would never run off and leave us to fend for ourselves." Adaline was convinced this would never happen.

S.W. was silently listening and he remained silent until Adaline questioned him.

"Isn't that right, S.W.?" Adaline wanted him to confirm her statement.

"Well, I..." S.W. was lost for words. Just at that moment Samuel and Mrs. Truby came into view and he was able to elude answering her question.

"S.W., are ye still here? Oliver sent word that if ye didn't hurry up ye could walk home!" Samuel laughed as he got in the buggy. "See, he's a turnin' the buggy 'round now!" Samuel pointed to their buggy in front of the church.

S.W. quickly helped Mrs. Truby in the buggy and replied, "Well then, I better hurry." S.W. ran to the front of the church where Oliver was already heading the buggy toward home. Charlotte rode up front with Oliver and S.W. jumped in the back with Amy Ann.

"Well, it's a good thing Gilbert is with the Donaldsons or there wouldn't be any room for you at all," said Amy Ann as she scooted over to make room for his long legs. "What took you so long? Were you with your sweetie?" Amy Ann teased.

S.W. seriously responded, "I was talking to Adaline and

Betsy. Betsy seems to be upset today."

Charlotte turned around in the buggy seat and yelled at him, "Well, who isn't upset? The preacher delivered very upsetting news! It's just a matter of time before enlistment posters get nailed up all over the county. I can just see the poster headlines…Wanted Volunteers for the Army! Get paid $13 per Month for Your Service! Aunt Sarah has received reports from Uncle Albert telling her all about the other Ohio counties enticing our young men to go to war."

"Just how do you know all this is true? Aunt Sarah has a way of making things sound…," S.W. hesitated, "worse than they really are."

"It's not hard to know all about it when Gilbert comes home raving about everything Mr. McClure and the Donaldsons fill his head full of!" Charlotte was enraged. "Gilbert is just wild with big ideas about fighting for the Union and I suppose you and Oliver helped with that!" Charlotte turned back around in the buggy seat.

"Now, don't come all unraveled, Charlotte," S.W. leaned forward in the buggy to speak. "You can't protect Gilbert forever!"

Charlotte was silent on the ride home, however, Amy Ann thought it was fitting to add her bit of information to the subject at hand.

"Aunt Sarah says that Governor Dennison is calling for

volunteers and he's going to start recruiting rapidly in our part of the state. Are you and Oliver going to join up?" Amy Ann looked at S.W. for an answer.

"Amy Ann, you don't need to worry," S.W. replied as he held her hand in a loving brotherly gesture.

Oliver slowed the buggy to a stop in front of the old log house. S.W. was the first to jump out. He stretched his long legs after having been cramped up in the back seat of the buggy, then he helped Amy Ann down. Charlotte declined his help. S.W. noticed a tear flow down her cheek when she looked at him.

Oliver announced that he was going to visit Aunt Sarah later in the day and Amy Ann quickly invited herself to go along.

"How about you, S.W.? Do you want to come along?" asked Oliver.

"Thanks, but I'm going over to the Trubys' to spend the afternoon with Adaline."

"Suit yourself, brother. You might miss out on seeing the lovely Miss Lily. I heard she came into town this week." Oliver was pleased to offer this tidbit of information.

"Oh, you got me mixed-up with Samuel, although I'll be sure to tell Samuel that Miss Lily requests his company." S.W. said.

Charlotte was standing on the porch listening to them

make plans when she decided to speak up.

"Oh, Oliver, I think I will go with you to visit Aunt Sarah. I need a change of company."

"Good, let's hurry and get a bite to eat and then we will be on our way," shouted Oliver as he jumped down from the buggy and tied the reins to the post.

Charlotte was looking forward to visiting with Aunt Sarah and making plans for a happy gathering as she thought it could well be the last time they would all be together.

Chapter Thirteen
The Gathering

Chairs and tables were brought out of Aunt Sarah's kitchen and arranged in the backyard amongst the flowers and under the shade trees in preparation for the gathering. Gilbert and Henry sat down on the garden bench to rest for a moment after helping bring the furniture outside. The delicious aroma of the many different foods cooking in the kitchen drifted outside.

"Smell that fried chicken, Henry?" Gilbert asked.

"I surely do and it smells mighty good," answered Henry.

"That's Mrs. Smith's secret recipe. First, she dips each piece in milk and then sprinkles salt and pepper all over it, then she dips it again in eggs and crumbs, then she fries it in a huge skillet of lard until it's nice and crispy." Gilbert was licking his lips.

Henry just shook his head at Gilbert as he jumped up from the bench to get back to work.

Miss Lily was placing tablecloths on the tables and Cora began arranging the tables with plates and dessert dishes. Charlotte and Amy Ann brought out the fancy teacups with matching saucers. Mrs. Smith carried out three different kinds of cakes: white cake, applesauce cake, and spice cake. The rest of the food would be brought out when the guests arrived.

"Everything seems to be in order," said Miss Lily.

"What do we do now?" Amy Ann inquired.

"Just wait on the guests to arrive," answered Miss Lily.

Charlotte and Amy Ann went around to sit on the front porch to greet their guests. It was to Charlotte's surprise when the preacher and his wife arrived first. Charlotte jumped up to welcome them.

"It's so nice of you to join us." Charlotte stepped down from the porch to greet them.

"Oh, we were delighted when we received your invitation," said the preacher's wife. She had a very pleasant and bubbly personality which seemed to match her short plump body. She promptly handed the basket of baked items she was carrying to Charlotte.

"Two loaves of baked bread," said the preacher's wife. "I always say you can never have enough bread."

"Yes, indeed," said Charlotte. "Thank you very much."

"We've been looking forward to coming all week," said the

preacher who was a middle-aged tall, thin man with wire rimmed glasses. He was the exact opposite of his wife although the two of them were both very articulated conversationalists which made Charlotte worry about how Miss Lily would get along with them. "Miss Lily really wasn't the church-going kind," Charlotte thought to herself as she swiftly moved ahead of them guiding them down the path of stepping stones that lead to the backyard.

They walked under the old-fashioned archway rose trellis which was covered with pale pink roses. They continued past brilliant colored hollyhocks, standing tall against the stone wall and finally they stopped by the herb garden where Miss Lily was directing Gilbert on where to place a few more chairs. Charlotte introduced the preacher and his wife to Miss Lily.

Miss Lily hastily offered them seats in the shade. "Miss Lily," the preacher was quick to inquire, "I don't believe we've seen you in our church before?" He looked at her over top of his wire rimmed glasses.

"Why no, Preacher Dunkin, I haven't had the pleasure. My home is in Cincinnati. I'm here visiting with Aunt Sarah and Uncle Albert for a few weeks."

"Oh, what a grand city! I just love Cincinnati!" the preacher's wife cheerfully exclaimed.

Miss Lily's attention was suddenly distracted when the Sheriff sneaked in behind her and kissed her on the cheek.

Preacher Dunkin and his wife were taken aback by the Sheriff's bold signs of affection.

"Oh, you startled me! I didn't know you were here." Miss Lily jumped up from her seat and gave him a big hug then she introduced Preacher Dunkin and his wife to the Sheriff.

"Good to meet you," said the Sheriff in his deep masculine voice. He shook hands with the Preacher and tipped his black slouch hat to the Preacher's wife before wandering off.

"You'll have to excuse the Sheriff; he just can't stay put for very long. Can I get you something to drink?" Miss Lily asked.

"That would be most kind of you," said the Preacher's wife.

"Please excuse me and I'll return quickly with drinks for both of you." Miss Lily hustled to get away as she sensed a Bible sermon coming. She saw Samuel standing in the kitchen doorway and rushed off in his direction.

"Samuel," she said as she approached, "It's so nice to see you again." She flashed him a smile while all the while her snappy brown eyes beheld his tan and muscled body.

Samuel offered his hand as she climbed the steps to enter the kitchen. He was thinking about the first time he had met her when she departed the train on that hot summer morning in Ottawa, when suddenly, Aunt Sarah rushed into the kitchen and interrupted his thoughts.

"Has anyone seen your Uncle Albert? Please, keep the

spirits away from him while the preacher is here. I've warned him not to touch a drop. I fear he hasn't listened!" Aunt Sarah was beside herself. She rubbed her forehead as though she had a headache. As she looked out the kitchen door she saw Uncle Albert and the Sheriff walking towards the Preacher with drinks in their hands. They were fast approaching Preacher Dunkin and his wife.

"Oh no, I fear the worst is about to happen. What shall I do?" Aunt Sarah stopped in her tracks and couldn't speak.

At that very moment, Gilbert and Cora stood in front of Preacher Dunkin and his wife, ready to serve them mugs filled with sassafras tea. Cora and Gilbert sat down with the preacher and his wife. Gilbert called out to Uncle Albert to sit on the empty chair next to him.

"Uncle Albert, sit here next to me!" Gilbert put his hand on the seat of the old wooden chair to further indicate the seating arrangement.

"Oh, there you are lad," said Uncle Albert as he sat down next to Gilbert and tipped his hat to greet the others.

The Sheriff sat down next to Preacher Dunkin's wife. The Preacher's wife was very cordial with the Sheriff. It wasn't long before the Sheriff felt comfortable and was telling tales of his wagon train days to his captive audience. Uncle Albert was just relaxed enough not to interrupt although he did whisper to Gilbert that he needed another drink.

"We're just 'bout ready to eat. Maybe you should wait a bit?" Gilbert suggested to Uncle Albert in a very low tone.

"Alright, alright, I can wait," whispered Uncle Albert as he peered into his empty mug.

Aunt Sarah was relieved to see that Uncle Albert was under control for now. She proceeded to hurry Mrs. Smith along to get the food on the tables and was most appreciative of Adaline, Betsy, and Mrs. Truby's help. Aunt Sarah soon announced that dinner was ready and everyone should take their seats at the tables. Preacher Dunkin stood and said a lengthy prayer before eating.

After dinner Gilbert kept Uncle Albert busy with a game of dominoes which they played on an old wooden barrel turned upside down. Aunt Sarah was thankful that Gilbert was keeping him occupied so she could converse with Preacher Dunkin and his wife. They sat on the front porch with some of the other guests to discuss the supplies needed for the field hospitals and Miss Lily joined them. She was well received by Preacher Dunkin and his wife once they learned of her involvement with the anti-slavery movement as well as her influence with others who would willingly contribute financially to help with food and medical supplies for the war.

Adaline, Betsy, and Mrs. Truby shied away from the group and withdrew to the kitchen to assist Mrs. Smith with cleaning up. Once the kitchen was cleaned, Adaline sneaked away with

S.W. to the back of the property near where Henry lived.

They slowly walked hand-in-hand down the footpath that led to Henry's little shack. S.W. and Adaline stopped to rest on an old log in the woods. Finally, they were alone in the stillness of the trees. They had much to talk about before S.W. signed his enlistment papers.

The front porch group meeting came to an end and most of the guests went home. Miss Lily found her way to the back of the house where she found Samuel. He was engaged in a game of horseshoes with Oliver, Gilbert, and the Sheriff. Miss Lily sat down with Uncle Albert and joined him in drinking a little of the apple brandy. The day was winding down and Miss Lily was feeling melancholy as she thought about the young men going off to war.

Samuel noticed Lily sitting with Uncle Albert. Samuel walked over and persuaded Uncle Albert to take a turn at playing horseshoes. Samuel took Uncle Albert's seat and pulled the chair closer to Lily.

"I finally have a chance to talk to ye," said Samuel as he leaned in closer to Lily. "It's mighty hard to just talk to ye with so many folks 'round all the time."

"Why Samuel, I didn't know you wanted to just talk to me." Lily gestured with both of her hands over her heart. "Oh… it gives me great pleasure to be near you, Samuel."

"Please, be serious Lily. Don't make a fool of me. I've given a lot of thought to this," said Samuel as he sat on the chair facing Lily.

Lily sat silently waiting for Samuel to continue.

"I'll be leavin' as soon as Governor Dennison gives the orders. Word is that Kentucky might not be able to stay neutral much longer. The Confederate troops are movin' into Kentucky and that will end their neutrality. Do ye know what that means, Lily? The Union must stand forever!"

Lily knew it was important for Samuel to be heard and so she remained silent waiting on him to speak his mind.

Samuel was looking into Lily's eyes and searching for just the right words to say. "I'm good with a rifle and I could be one of those sharpshooters. I can ride a horse pretty good and they want recruits for the cavalry. The point is the Union wants volunteers immediately and I'll be leavin' next month."

Lily touched Samuel's arm in a loving manner.

"So, Lily, I might not get another chance to tell ye that I think ye is the prettiest woman I ever met. I have a lot of respect for ye."

"Oh, Samuel, don't talk that way. You are brave and you will return and I'll be right here waiting."

"I have a favor to ask. Will ye look after Adaline and Betsy and Mama from time to time?"

"You know I will." Lily got up from the chair and took Samuel by the hand. "Let's go for a walk."

They strolled past the herb garden and under the rose trellis archway until they reached the stepping stone path which led to the front porch. They sat together on the porch until Mrs. Truby came outside to send Samuel to find Adaline.

"Samuel, we need to get home now. We have chores to do. Will ye go in search of Adaline?" Mrs. Truby sat down with Miss Lily while Samuel raced off to get Adaline.

"Miss Lily, ye know my Samuel tis a good lad, but I fear he will be leavin' us. I hope ye not be leading him on to believe ye care for him."

"I have faith in Samuel and I care very much for him," said Lily.

"Ye shall have faith in the Lord, Miss Lily." Mrs. Truby corrected her and proceeded to say, "Maybe ye be comin' to church on Sunday?" Mrs. Truby asked before going back in the house to bid farewell to Aunt Sarah. Adaline had just stepped up onto the porch and heard the tail end of the conversation between Miss Lily and Mrs. Truby.

Miss Lily smiled at Mrs. Truby, however she didn't confirm her attendance at church on Sunday.

"Oh, Mama," Adaline announced. "Samuel went to get the buggy."

Miss Lily gave her attention to Adaline while they waited on Samuel to bring the buggy around. During the course of their conversation Adaline confirmed that S.W. and Samuel would be leaving next month.

It had been a very successful gathering at Aunt Sarah's place. Now that everyone had gone home, the big house seemed lonely. The clean-up was done and the furniture was placed back in the house. Uncle Albert was settled in for the evening. Miss Lily and Cora retired to their rooms upstairs. Henry had finished up the chores and gone to his shack in the woods. Aunt Sarah sat alone in the parlor reflecting on the events of the day before going to bed. "Things are changing and not for the good," Aunt Sarah thought to herself.

Chapter Fourteen
The Ohio Send-off

*crowd gathered at Kalida to give the enlisted men a formal send-off as they departed for their training camp in the Fifty-Seventh Volunteer Regiment, Company A, from Putnam County. The Regiment was sent to Camp Vance in Findlay. It took time for S.W. and Samuel to adjust to camp life, but being away from home and family was the hardest adjustment of all. The few letters that did arrive were short and only informed the family that their regiment was being sent to Camp Chase near Columbus for more training.

After reading the letters that S.W. sent home Oliver surmised, "I reckon they can't tell us much. Most likely they don't know where they'll be sent to after training at Camp Chase.

"Well, I do hope S.W. gets a furlough home after he completes his training at Camp Chase," said Charlotte.

"Certainly, they wouldn't send him out to battle without

coming home first." Amy Ann looked worrisome. "Aunt Sarah says it could take up to seven months or more before a furlough might be issued. That seems like a very long time."

Silence filled the kitchen following Amy Ann's statement as there was nothing encouraging to be said about the soldiers at Camp Vance.

A few days later after receiving the first letter from S.W. a note was found on the kitchen table from Gilbert telling them that he had run off to enlist.

"It's just like Gilbert to run off in the middle of the night without having to say goodbye," said Charlotte.

Charlotte was angry and now she was concerned because Oliver was the only one left to work the farm and that might be short lived too as he was hinting of marrying the woman he had met at the church last year. He had been sneaking off to visit her more often and was openly expressing his fondness for her.

Oliver was becoming angry after giving more thought to Gilbert running away. He pounded his fist on the kitchen table and shouted, "That Gilbert was needed more at home than in the Army and now his foolishness will surely get him killed."

Charlotte was shocked by Oliver's reaction as she stopped and turned around to look at him. Amy Ann sat at the table sobbing and Charlotte tried to comfort her.

"Really, Oliver! Why would you say such a thing? Life is

hard enough to deal with without saying such things!"

"I'm sorry Charlotte," replied Oliver as he put on his coat and stormed outside.

Unbeknownst to the family, Gilbert had joined up with some rowdy young men as he was in route to sign up. Gilbert's newfound ruffian friends told him they too were going to enlist. They instructed him to hide in the empty stock car with them as the train was slowly starting off from the station. Gilbert jumped on board. Gilbert and his friends journeyed along sitting on the floor of dirty straw. Gilbert told them that first he had to pay a visit to a man in Cincinnati and that man, being Mr. Johnson, the nephew to Mrs. Johnson, needed to be taught a lesson. They were good listeners and Gilbert was impressed that he was being taken seriously for a change.

The train continued slowly rolling down the tracks when one of the young ruffians asked, "Where might this fella live? Ye got the street and number?"

Gilbert was slow to respond which angered Gilbert's new friend. "Well, have you got it or not?"

"I got the street name and number right here," Gilbert said as he pulled it out of his coat pocket and read it out loud. "90 Wade Street," said Gilbert. "Do you fellas know how to get there?"

Gilbert looked at the rough bunch and silently wondered, "What have I got myself into?"

"Well... let me think on that," said the oldest of the bunch as he rubbed his chin. "Could be we could help ye. This man ye speak of, might he be a man of prosperity?"

"Yes, as a matter of fact he is! Now, you see it doesn't rightfully belong to him. He is guilty of forcin' himself on my good friend, Cora, and he has falsely taken her home and everything she owns."

"Ye be callin' him a rapist and a thief! This, Mr. Johnson, ye say his name is Johnson? He took advantage of your friend? This friend, might she be your sweetheart?"

"No! She's a good woman, that's all. She's a fine woman!" Gilbert was defensive.

There was a moment of silence among the group as they waited on the leader of the bunch to speak.

"What say ye boys, should we help Gilbert teach this man a lesson he'll not soon forget?"

"Ye be sure he's a man of prosperity who lives in a fine home?" asked one of the others who was relaxing in a bed of straw, "Cincinnati is a bit of a ways to go."

"I'm sure," replied Gilbert. "I told you that it doesn't rightfully belong to him. It belongs to my friend."

"Gilbert, we heard what ye have to say, now prepare to jump off the train before it comes to a stop or we all be runnin' from the law," the oldest of the bunch gave the command.

Gilbert and the oldest of the bunch located the house at

90 Wade Street just before dusk and surveyed the surroundings as the others split-up and waited nearby so as not to be noticed.

"Gilbert, ye wait here in the alley while I go knock on the door."

"What are you goin' to knock on the door for?" asked Gilbert with surprise.

"To make sure it be the scandalous Mr. Johnson ye seek out and to know if he has any company in the house. This ain't me first time doin' this." And off he strutted up to the front door and proceeded banging the metal door rapper until someone came to the door.

The door opened wide as Mr. Johnson stood in the doorway looking very stern and ready to slam the door shut in the young man's face, but the intruder was a fast talker and an accomplished impostor.

"My, kind sir, won't ye please spare just a wee bit of ye time? I can make ye yard and home be the most beautiful on the street. I have lots of experience and all me work is for just a wee bit of change. What be your name, kind sir?"

"My name is Johnson and I don't need a yard keeper!" shouted Mr. Johnson with hatred in his eyes.

"Well, maybe the lady of the house..."

"There is no lady of the house, now get out of here before I call the law on you. You beggar!"

"Forgive me sir and goodnight to ye." The young man tipped his hat and stepped ever so lightly down the steps with a smirk formed on his lips as he made plans to gain entry into house.

The young master of deceit went back to meet with Gilbert to gather the others to plan the break-in and then wait for the perfect timing to enter the home.

A few weeks following the break-in, Aunt Sarah and Cora received a letter from their lawyer, Mr. Hayes, which explained in detail the break-in and murder of Mr. Johnson. They were surprised to learn of his death and only assumed it had something to do with his position in the KGC, (Knights of the Golden Circle) and that of being a Southern sympathizer. The family never had reason to entertain thoughts of Gilbert being an accomplice in the break-in or in the murder of Mr. Johnson. In fact, it was just a week earlier that a letter was received from Gilbert telling the family of his enlistment and how much he liked the men in his camp. Gilbert didn't want them to ever learn of his involvement with the break-in or that he was a witness to the murder. It was of no surprise to Gilbert when the young bunch of ruffians didn't enlist and instead made fun of him for doing so as they made off with money and valuables from the house.

Chapter Fifteen
Fall 1861
Death Comes Too Soon

$\mathcal{G}$t was hard work for the Truby women to keep up with the daily chores since Samuel had enlisted three months ago. As always Mrs. Truby and her daughters relied heavily on prayer.

It was Friday and Mrs. Truby, Betsy, and Adaline were busy making pies for the yearly fall gathering which was due to take place on Saturday night at the Donaldsons'. Adaline was daydreaming as she often found herself doing since S.W.'s departure. She was dreaming of S.W. as though he were standing right next to her and she could hear his voice whispering the words in her ear, "I love you, Adaline," then suddenly there was a loud knock on the door. Oliver was standing there with a letter in his hand and a smile on his face when Adaline opened the door. He reminded Adaline of S.W. She wished in her heart that it might be S.W. instead of Oliver.

"Oh, Oliver, please come in," said Adaline. "Come, come

in and sit at the table. Will ye have a bite to eat?"

Mrs. Truby motioned with her arms for him to come sit as she pulled out a chair for him.

"No thank you. I can't stay. I just came from the post office. I knew Adaline would want this letter. I'm sorry there weren't any letters from Samuel today." Oliver continued to stand near the door.

"Tis alright. Samuel writes to Miss Lily and she keeps us informed," Mrs. Truby smiled at Oliver.

Adaline quickly took the letter, removed it from the envelope and proceeded to read it out loud.

My Dearest Adaline,

I am still at Camp Vance. Things are mighty slow around here. It took some time getting used to all the army commands that we must remember. Word is we might be moving out in January to Camp Chase in Columbus. We are still waiting on word from the Governor before we can leave.

Samuel sends his love to the family. He says to tell you all he misses you and wishes he were home to eat the good food that his mama cooks.

I made friends with a fine young soldier, named Wiser and it so happens that he lives near Kalida. I think Betsy might take a liking to him.

Tell Betsy I plan on bringing him home to meet her when we get a furlough.

Not much to tell except I sure do miss the family and most of all you, Adaline.

Love you,

S.W.

"I'd say S.W. sure is short on words with not much going on at Camp Vance," Oliver said as Adaline folded the letter and put it back in the envelope.

"Although, it sure sounds like there could be a fella for Betsy and since S.W. approves of him I'd judge him to be a good fella." Oliver couldn't resist teasing Betsy just a little.

Betsy was sitting at the table peeling apples when she looked up at Oliver and replied, "Tis not amusing! S.W. must think I not be able to find a man! Really, ye should tell S.W. to stop such foolishness!"

Mrs. Truby smiled at Betsy and said, "Betsy, I do think it might be nice for ye to meet him. Ye could at least consider it." Mrs. Truby wiped her hands on her apron as she went to gather more ingredients for the pies.

"Well, it could be a long time before the men have a furlough approved so you have plenty of time to think on it," said Oliver as he stood there grinning at Betsy.

Betsy was silent, but secretly she wondered what the young man might look like and what it would be like to have a beau of her own.

Oliver just stood there grinning and watching Betsy's face turn red from embarrassment before he said goodbye.

"Thank ye, Oliver for stoppin' by and for helpin' out. Will ye be bringin' your girl to the fall gatherin'?" Mrs. Truby inquired.

"I surely will." Oliver's voice was full of pride as he thought of showing-off his soon to be bride.

"Oh, good," said Adaline. "We look forward to meetin' her," Adaline smiled happily.

Oliver headed back home to inform Charlotte and Amy Ann of the latest news. They were always excited to receive letters from S.W. and Samuel.

Once Oliver got home, he immediately went in the house to rest by the fireplace, where he told Charlotte and Amy Ann of the letter.

"Oh, good news! Is Betsy excited to meet soldier Wiser? And what about Samuel? Have there been any reports about how soon they will be moving out?" asked Charlotte.

"Charlotte, I can only answer one question at a time. No, I reckon Samuel sends most of his letters to Miss Lily. The camp is waiting on word from the Governor before they can move out. S.W. thinks it will be in January," replied Oliver as he took a sip of coffee and then continued talking. "Betsy got a little riled about S.W. bringing someone home on furlough for her to meet. The funny thing is that Mrs. Truby thinks it's a grand idea," said Oliver. He paused to take another sip of coffee. "The Trubys are busy baking plenty of pies to take over to the Donaldsons' tomorrow night. It looks like you girls better be getting busy. Tomorrow is Saturday," Oliver reminded them.

Oliver finished his coffee and prepared to go outside when a thought came to him on his way out the door, "Oh say, Charlotte, that fella that Aunt Sarah introduced you to might just have a surprise for you come Saturday night."

"I don't know what you're talking about!" Charlotte sounded annoyed by his sudden comment.

Amy Ann raised her eyebrows in surprise and said, "I reckon you will find out tomorrow night. I just love surprises! Don't you Charlotte?"

"Do you know something about this?" Charlotte asked Amy Ann.

"I can't say. I made a promise to Aunt Sarah not to tell."

"Alright, since you made a promise I will just have to wait," responded Charlotte as she gathered up the baking supplies and placed them on the table.

The Saturday night gathering proved to be a much needed celebration with Aunt Sarah, Miss Lily, and Cora being the first to arrive. Mr. Donaldson had cleared out the barn where they stored apples and made cider as it had a thick wooden floor and proved to be perfect for dancing and entertaining. Charlotte played the fiddle and an older Donaldson boy played the mouth harp as many folks joined in clapping their hands and tapping their feet to keep time to the music. Miss Lily's beautiful singing voice was an added attraction. Many of the younger ones joined in the dancing and singing. The lively music brought the old barn to life. Even Mrs. Truby and Mrs. Donaldson participated in dancing with the younger children. It was almost a perfect ending for the fall harvest had it not been for the absence of some young men.

Most folks went home early as the fall night air was getting colder, although not before congratulating Oliver and his girl on their wedding plans as well as to congratulate Charlotte and Mr. Kitchen, who also made an unexpected wedding announcement.

"Oh, I do love weddings! You are all invited to my place for the blissful events! I will notify you when dates have been established," Aunt Sarah exclaimed as she stood in front of the small crowd of intent listeners.

Charlotte appeared to be embarrassed as she looked down at the floor blushing, however Mr. Kitchen was very much the gentleman as he graciously accepted everyone's congratulations.

Cora was the one who really took the center of attention throughout the evening with many inquisitive folks questioning her move to Cincinnati. Miss Lily was right there with her to inform them of the magnificent house and the potential business location it offered. Cora, on the other hand, wasn't so eager to divulge so much information. Cora frowned at Miss Lily as she went about busying herself at the food table.

There was much talk of S.W. and Samuel and of course everyone wanted to know of Gilbert's whereabouts, but not much could be told about Gilbert as the family unfortunately awaited more news. All and all the evening had been very eventful and folks reported having a pleasant evening as they departed for home.

November 1861

Oliver was spending more time away from home preparing a place for his new bride. Aunt Sarah sent Henry over daily to help the girls. Henry had gone home before dark, leaving Charlotte and Amy Ann alone. They were relaxing by the fireplace when they heard the dogs barking and then someone knocking on the door.

"Who could that be?" asked Amy Ann.

"I'll go see who is at the door," said Charlotte as she quickly got up to unbolt the door.

"Who is calling?" Charlotte questioned before completely

unlatching the door. They were much more cautious now as there were many drifters traveling through and Charlotte and Amy Ann were alone most of the time in the evening.

"It be Mr. McClure. I come to deliver a letter!" he called out.

Charlotte opened the door and stood face-to-face with Mr. McClure. "Mr. McClure! Won't you come in? Can I get you a drink?" Charlotte offered.

Mr. McClure thrust the letter into Charlotte's hand and then took a seat by the fire. "No drinks for me. Thank ye."

Charlotte opened the letter. It was from a military field hospital in Kentucky.

"It says here that Gilbert took sick and died from the fever!" Charlotte calmed herself after giving way to tears which streamed down her face.

"I'll read it to you," said Charlotte. The letter was addressed to Oliver and written as follows:

Oliver Jeffrey
Franconia Post Office
Putnam County, Ohio
    I am writing with humble regrets to inform you of the death of Private Gilbert Jeffrey of the 38th Regiment, Ohio Volunteer Infantry, Company F. Several of our soldiers have died from the measles. When Gilbert took sick and came down with the

fever he asked me to write to his family.

We are using the church as our hospital and it is crowded with our sick and wounded soldiers. Many of us and the preacher prayed over Gilbert. We truly thought he would pull through, Gilbert, being such a young lad and all. I reckon all the cold nights and food being scarce in the camp was all too much for him to endure. Gilbert wanted you to know how he loved you all. We buried him under a crab apple tree near the church and placed on it a wooden cross.

With all due respect and many regrets,
Private Milton 38th Regiment
Ohio Volunteer Infantry, Company F

Charlotte slumped down on an old wooden chair as Amy Ann knelt on the floor placing her head on Charlotte's lap. Charlotte stroked Amy Ann's long blond hair. Amy Ann sobbed. After all that had happened, Charlotte was too stunned to cry.

"I sure am sorry to bring such bad news to ye. Gilbert will surely be missed. I'm thinkin' I best deliver ye into town to ye Aunt Sarah's."

"Thank you, Mr. McClure. I'll just leave this letter on the table for Oliver to read when he gets home."

When they arrived at Aunt Sarah's they were welcomed and comforted with open arms. Amy Ann ran the short distance to Henry's shack to tell him of the dreadful news. Henry and Amy Ann walked back to the big house with the light of the moon to guide them. They sat in the kitchen reminiscing about all the good times they shared with Gilbert. Miss Lily and Aunt Sarah stayed with Charlotte and Amy Ann late into the night, unable to sleep or find peace following the news of Gilbert's death.

"Tomorrow I will send for the preacher and speak with him about having a few words said during church services. It just wouldn't be right not to. Oh, and I must get a message to your Uncle Albert," said Aunt Sarah with her voice quivering as she tried to hold back the tears.

"Oh, how I do wish we could bring Gilbert home to be buried with our loved ones," Aunt Sarah softly said.

"I wish Cora were here with us! Can you send for her? Please Aunt Sarah, send for Cora!" Amy Ann begged.

"Of course, I will notify her. Remember, she just recently arrived back home in Cincinnati and she needs to stay there and protect her property from thieves. Oh, woe with me, there simply is so much to do!" Aunt Sarah sorrowfully answered.

Miss Lily announced, "I will travel to Cincinnati and personally tell Cora. She will need some company when she hears of this dreadful event."

Oliver arrived home the next morning and rushed to get the chores done so he could travel into town to be with the family. He, too, was shaken by the sudden news of Gilbert's death; however, he was surprised when he arrived at Aunt Sarah's that everyone seemed to have accepted Gilbert's death. It was not being able to bring Gilbert home for a proper burial that was the most troublesome and weighed heavy on their hearts.

"Oh, don't cry, Aunt Sarah. Gilbert wouldn't want you to cry for him. Gilbert was jolly most of the time and he wouldn't take kindly to your crying." Amy Ann tried to sooth Aunt Sarah's aching heart as well as her own.

Everyone was gathered in the kitchen when Henry brought in more firewood. He carefully stacked it on the floor by the fireplace. Miss Lily was making plans to take the train to Cincinnati and stay with Cora for a few weeks. In spite of all the sadness that came from Gilbert's death, Charlotte found herself entertaining thoughts and making plans for her wedding, which she hoped would take place sometime after the new year. Oliver curtly reminded them of his own soon to be marriage and that he planned on moving to the next county with his new bride after the first of the year. The room quickly became silent following his announcement of an early marriage and plenty of questions ensued.

"You never mentioned you were getting married so soon. We've hardly had time to prepare," Charlotte protested.

"Just what will we do with the farm? We can't manage the

farm alone!" Amy Ann joined in protesting Oliver's early marriage.

"Oh, dear me, how can you be entertaining thoughts of matrimony and we haven't even had an opportunity to call for the preacher much less say our goodbyes and hold a service for Gilbert! We simply must have a period of mourning for Gilbert! Girls, you must wear your black clothes. Don't even think of your clothes of merry matrimony!" Aunt Sarah was most upset as she hurried Henry off to fetch the preacher.

The family observed the customary period of mourning for young Gilbert. Friends and neighbors came by to pay their respects to the family. At church the preacher gave a lengthy sermon as Aunt Sarah inconspicuously gave him a large contribution to be spent on field hospital supplies. Uncle Albert traveled home to be with the family, whereas, Miss Lily traveled to Cincinnati to stay with Cora. Cora was indeed very grieved after hearing of Gilbert's death and she found Miss Lily's company to be very comforting.

Chapter Sixteen
January-February 1862

Oliver moved to the next county with his new bride and a short time later Charlotte married and moved to Greensburg township. Amy Ann went to live with Aunt Sarah. The old farmhouse was now empty, but not for long, as the oldest Donaldson boy and his young wife and family were set on moving in.

"You may as well move in and keep up the place. It will be three years before S.W. returns and can do the farming again," Aunt Sarah reasoned with the hardworking young farmer as they stood on the porch of the old log house. It was a chilly February morning and they were dressed in their warm winter clothes.

The young farmer and his family were thankful they had reached an agreement even if it was only for three years. Everyone went away satisfied as it would soon be time to plow and plant the fields.

Henry drove the buggy back into town. Amy Ann met Aunt Sarah at the backdoor and excitedly hurried her into the house where she handed over a letter from Miss Lily. Still wearing her winter coat, Aunt Sarah sat down at the kitchen table to read the letter. Mrs. Smith and Amy Ann sat down with her and anxiously waited to hear the latest report as all of Miss Lily's letters were very informative and gave a glimpse of what life must be like in Cincinnati. Amy Ann was very attentive as she listened with great anticipation.

Dear Aunt Sarah,

I am writing to inform you of the latest events in Cincinnati. Cora and I are getting along wondrously. Cora needs me with her in this grand old house! There are far too many men of an unscrupulous nature running about the city. There seems to be increased drunkenness and disorderly conduct not to mention thievery, however, you need not worry about us as I have called upon two of my old friends to escort us when we need to go to the market or mercantile store.

Oh, and speaking of the market, there seems to be a good supply of produce and the prices remain affordable, however, the price of meat has risen.

The weather was still very cold when I ventured

out yesterday, however, I was able to view one of the Cavalry Regiments pass through the city and it was a fine display of our gallant soldiers. I do believe there are thousands of horses in this city. There seems to have been a major purchase of horses for Government use. There also seems to be reports of treason for supplying horses and mules to the Rebels.

Oh, you do know that the Government put a stop to all travelers trying to go South. I do think the orders are being strictly enforced as Southern Sympathizers attempt to aid the Rebels. And now, I must tell you the good news about Cora. I introduced Cora to some lovely people who are now living here as boarders.

These good folks are simply very charming and they can well afford to pay a handsome price for a room and meals. The word is spreading that Cora is a remarkable cook and that the house offers clean and spacious rooms for rent.

I have just recently made a chance encounter with some old theatrical acquaintances and I am hopeful of working once again in the theater. I am so looking forward to purchasing a new dress for my first performance.

Before I close my letter, I am anxious to tell you that the ladies Of the Church where Cora and I attend, propose that each one of us knit woolen yarn socks for our soldiers. Dare I impose on you and Amy Ann to knit a few stockings?

Yours most truly,
Lily

"Good heavens! You know Lily can't knit! I reckon she wants us to do it for her," Mrs. Smith complained and then continued to sum up the letter. "Well, Miss Lily is certainly the most enterprising young woman that I ever had the chance to meet," stated Mrs. Smith as she stood up from the table. "She surely is eager to undertake new projects. She may be a little too eager for Cora's liking," Mrs. Smith reasoned.

"I know Lily can be a bit forward, but I do think she has Cora's best interest at heart. Cora has a mind of her own and she can speak it when she wants to," Aunt Sarah replied.

"I'm so happy that Miss Lily is getting back into the theater and that everything is going well for her and Cora," said Amy Ann as she left the kitchen to go upstairs.

"I hear tell that the fighting is getting fierce in Kentucky and Tennessee," Mrs. Smith spoke up after Amy Ann had left the room. "Reports are circulating that the boys from the 57th Ohio Infantry are moving up the Tennessee River and they are to accompany the gunboats and travel on to Mississippi.

That's what I overheard some of the men saying when I was at McClure's General Store this morning."

"I've heard the same reports Mrs. Smith and I know it's not looking good." Aunt Sarah couldn't hide the worried look on her face.

"I heard tell that Betsy has a collection of letters from Private Wiser," Mrs. Smith continued to report. "He must spend all his spare time writing letters to her."

"I do believe Private Wiser is a good match for Betsy. His letters are that of a gentleman, at least that's what Mrs. Truby proudly tells everyone," Mrs. Smith confirmed the latest news.

Amy Ann was overly curious as she came back into the kitchen and overheard the conversation. "Are the letters really sweetheart letters? I mean does he write sweet things?"

"Amy Ann, I really think you ought not pry into Betsy's affairs. Betsy is much too modest to reveal such matters," Aunt Sarah responded.

"I hope he proposes matrimony when he meets her! She is very beautiful. I just love her long dark curly hair." Amy Ann rambled on about Adaline and Betsy getting married. "Oh, I just had the most wonderful thought. Maybe Betsy and Adaline could have a double wedding?"

Aunt Sarah politely interrupted Amy Ann to ask her to help Mrs. Smith in the kitchen with the baking.

"Young lady, I do think you need to practice cooking and

baking so you can get yourself a nice young man someday," Aunt Sarah patted her on the shoulder.

The past few months had suddenly taken a toll on Aunt Sarah has she had tried to conceal her true feelings over the loss of Gilbert. "Someone has to be strong," she thought to herself.

Aunt Sarah got up to poke at the logs in the fireplace to get the fire burning better. Soon the flames were giving off more heat and the room was glowing from the orange and red dancing flames. Aunt Sarah was thinking of Gilbert and missing him terribly, but then her mind shifted to S.W. and Samuel.

"The mail surely is slow. Tomorrow maybe a letter will come from S.W. or Samuel?" Aunt Sarah suddenly found herself saying her thoughts out loud. "Tomorrow will bring good news."

When the mail arrived, it did not prove to be good news, rather it was news of yet another death. Samuel had been killed on the battlefield of Shiloh, Tennessee in late March of 1862. Mrs. Truby was devastated when she learned of the tragic death of her only son. Betsy and Adaline mourned over the loss of their brother. Adaline, who was usually full of hope and promises of a brighter day coming was now finding it hard to cope with Samuel's death.

Miss Lily remained in Cincinnati after learning of the

battle in Shiloh. She had Aunt Sarah check on the Trubys periodically and to let her know when they were in need.

Chapter Seventeen
January – March 1864

"Aunt Sarah! Aunt Sarah! Someone is pounding on the front door!" Amy Ann called out as she entered the bedroom where Aunt Sarah was sound asleep. Aunt Sarah was startled by Amy Ann's sudden entrance and she immediately sat on the edge of the bed.

"Well, for heaven's sake! Who could it be?" Aunt Sarah jumped up and covered herself with her robe and proceeded to light a lamp as she and Amy Ann slowly descended the stairs.

"Who is there?" Aunt Sarah called out.

"It's S.W. and I've brought Private Wiser with me!"

Aunt Sarah unlatched the door and opened it wide to shine the light on them. "Come in!" Aunt Sarah joyfully welcomed them.

"What a surprise!" Exclaimed Amy Ann as she hugged and kissed her brother for the first time in three years.

"Aunt Sarah and Amy Ann, this is Private Wiser. He's the fella I want Betsy to meet. I'm sure you've heard about him," S.W. said.

"Yes, we've had the pleasure of hearing all about him from the many letters Betsy has received." Amy Ann was quick to answer as she observed how fine a soldier Wiser looked even though his uniform was worn and tattered.

"It's nice to meet you Private Wiser," Aunt Sarah said as she held her hand out to greet him and suggested they go into the kitchen for something to eat.

"I'm sorry to disturb you this late at night, Aunt Sarah. I hope you don't mind if we rest here?" S.W. asked.

"You are welcome here anytime and you need not ask. There is hot water on the stove if you care to wash-up," suggested Aunt Sarah.

We are so thankful to be home on furlough," said S.W. as he was the first to sit down at the table after washing-up. Once he was seated he continued speaking.

"I'm sorry to tell you that we have orders to move further south when we return to camp."

"Return to camp? Whatever do you mean?" Aunt Sarah was dismayed.

"Aunt Sarah, I've reenlisted as have most all of the men," S.W. answered her.

"Well, let us not think of that now," Aunt Sarah demanded

as she began preparing a little something to eat.

S.W. and Private Wiser were grateful to be received so graciously at such a late hour as was evident by the way they consumed the food that Aunt Sarah laid out before them.

Amy Ann sat down at the table to inform the young soldiers of all the recent reports and rumors.

"There simply is so much to tell you!" Amy Ann was filled with young enthusiasm.

"So, I reckon Miss Lily will be making her home with Cora for a spell. Miss Lily, she likes living in the city." S. W. pondered over all that Amy Ann had repeated from Miss Lily's letters. S.W. was quiet after that as he sipped the hot cider and listened to the others talk.

Amy Ann replied to S.W.'s statement, "Yes, Miss Lily surely knows her way around Cincinnati! I suppose she will continue staying on with Cora since she is going back to the theater. It's all so exciting!"

"Please S.W., tell us about your travels?" Amy Ann asked.

"Amy Ann, I reckon it would be best not to speak of it," answered S.W.

"Well, Miss Amy Ann," Private Wiser responded, "I suppose you would like to hear about the beautiful Tennessee mountains, the rivers and streams that run through it. I'm sorry to say that right now, the beauty of it is mired by the war."

"Amy Ann, this is not the time to be asking questions," warned Aunt Sarah.

"I'm sorry." Amy Ann quickly apologized.

"I suppose you plan on meeting up with Betsy tomorrow?" Aunt Sarah followed up with asking the question of Private Wiser.

"I sure do hope so, ma'am. It will be a privilege to meet Betsy after hearing so much about her."

Amy Ann reacted excitedly, "I wish I could be there when you meet her! Aunt Sarah, you don't suppose...?"

"Absolutely not, Amy Ann. That wouldn't be proper!" Aunt Sarah scolded Amy Ann as her eyebrows moved in an upward motion.

It didn't take long for S.W. and Private Wiser to finish eating and Aunt Sarah noticed how very weary they looked.

"You must be very tired from your trip. I will show you to your room."

"Thank you kindly, ma'am. You are most hospitable," replied Private Wiser.

"I sure am sorry to impose on you like this, Aunt Sarah," S.W. apologized again as he followed her up the stairs.

"You need not worry yourself over it. I'm just so happy you came home. Please, get a goodnight's sleep," said Aunt Sarah and then she and Amy Ann kissed him goodnight.

The next day the young soldiers drove the horse and

buggy out to the farm. Mrs. Truby, Adaline, and Betsy embraced S.W. with love and Betsy finally got to meet Private Wiser.

While they were on furlough, Betsy and the young soldier enjoyed the next few weeks getting better acquainted, all the while, Adaline and S.W. spent all their spare time together. The time went by fast as Adaline counted the days when they would be leaving.

Aunt Sarah planned a surprise party for the young soldiers before their furlough was up. When they arrived at Aunt Sarah's front door Miss Lily was the first to greet them.

"Lily, I thought I would never see you again," S.W. surprisingly found himself saying.

"Don't be silly. I would never let you leave without seeing you off," she whispered softly and kissed him on the cheek. "And this must be Private Wiser, whom we have heard so much about. I am so very glad to finally meet you." Miss Lily offered her hand to him.

"Come in! Come in! Come in the house! Don't just stand there all day!" Uncle Albert demanded.

"Oh, Uncle Albert, be kind to our men in blue," said Lily as she flashed Uncle Albert a smile.

"Come in!" Uncle Albert shouted. "Come in and enjoy some good food and drinks!" Uncle Albert embraced S.W. and gave a good hearty handshake to Private Wiser.

"It's good to meet you," said Private Wiser.

"It's good to meet you too, Private Wiser," Uncle Albert spoke very loudly as though he were hard of hearing.

"Yes, you young soldiers are looking good in spite of all you been through. I do my best to keep up on all the latest news and reports of our Union troops. Our Union Army is doing a fine job and we certainly hope it will all be over soon. Now, join me and the Sheriff in the parlor!"

Miss Lily escorted S.W. and Private Wiser to their seats and delivered drinks to them. Uncle Albert removed his long-stemmed pipe and tobacco from the pipe stand and the sheriff found the box of stogies which was on the bookcase. S.W. declined smoking, though Private Wiser readily accepted a stogie when the Sheriff offered it. It wasn't long before the room was filled with tobacco smoke and loud conversation.

Mrs. Truby remained in the kitchen with Mrs. Smith and Aunt Sarah while Amy Ann, Adaline and Betsy joined Miss Lily in the parlor. Miss Lily sat down to play the piano and invited S.W.to play his mouth harp. S.W. carried his mouth harp in his pocket ever since he had enlisted. Amy Ann picked up the fiddle and together they produced some lively music which seemed to drown out any thoughts of Gilbert and Samuel of which no one dared to speak.

As more company arrived Betsy and Private Wiser wandered off somewhere within the crowded house. Before the meal was served Private Wiser managed to discuss with Betsy the possibility of matrimony. It was to Betsy's delight to hear him speak the words and she readily accepted his offer.

Just a short time later, Charlotte and her husband arrived with Oliver and his wife coming in behind. They brought gifts of food and drinks to share. The house was soon filled with gaiety as Uncle Albert had passed around the apple brandy. As usual he poured rum in the punchbowl. It wasn't until the meal was served that he produced the pink sparkling Catawba wine.

Uncle Albert came to the table with a bottle in each hand and proclaimed with a husky drunken voice, "We shall drink the most divine tasting wine ever to be produced in the Ohio River Valley!" Uncle Albert held the bottles up and gently waved them in the air.

"Here, Uncle Albert," said Oliver as he reached for the bottles, "let me help you with that."

Oliver then took charge of opening the wine and gently poured it into the delicate glasses. This was the perfect timing to proclaim a wedding engagement and ceremony as S.W. stood up to announce his plans to marry Adaline. Private Wiser also took the liberty to announce his betrothal to Betsy. The guests rejoiced with much pleasure after hearing of the planned double wedding.

It proved to be a joyful reunion with Aunt Sarah helping

Betsy and Adaline make wedding plans for March 8, 1864. Aunt Sarah cordially invited everyone to attend the ceremony at the church which would be followed with cake and refreshments at her house. The wedding celebration would be bittersweet as S.W. and Private Wiser prepared to depart a few days after the wedding ceremony.

S.W. tossed and turned as he tried to get some sleep the night before leaving. His thoughts drifted back to Kentucky and Tennessee where the 57th had accompanied the gunboats and transports on the Tennessee River. Frightful thoughts rambled on in his head as he tried to get to sleep, still his mind would not obey his commands and the sweet restful sleep didn't come. Finally, just as he started to drift off, flashes of the Union troops destroying the Confederate railroads raced through his mind. And there it was again, the 57th Regiment traveling through Kentucky, Tennessee, Mississippi, Arkansas, and Louisiana, joining up with the troops being led by Union General William T. Sherman to fight the Rebels. In his mind, he traveled back to late April 1863 when the 57th joined in General Ulysses S. Grant's advance on Vicksburg; to July 4th, 1863 when the Vicksburg's Confederates surrendered to the Union. All these thoughts of horrendous skirmishes and battles raced through S.W.'s mind. He knew he could never tell his little sister, Amy Ann, or anyone else for that matter, of his travels; it would stay forever in his mind.

Finally, when morning came and it was time to leave, sorrow filled Aunt Sarah's house. Aunt Sarah had instructed Mrs. Smith to prepare a gunnysack filled with food for the young soldiers to take with them on their way back to camp. Adaline and Betsy had great difficulty letting go as they stood on the front porch of Aunt Sarah's house.

"Adaline, you are the love of my life," S.W. whispered in her ear before stepping down off from the porch.

"God be with ye," Adaline responded as she tried not to cry in front of him.

Private Wiser was in the yard waiting on S.W. as he was not especially good at saying goodbyes and he knew they needed to get moving. He had already privately said his goodbyes to Betsy and he wanted to avoid any sorrowful delays.

Chapter Eighteen
A Letter to Betsy

When S.W. and his good friend Wiser arrived back at camp they joined the troops to move further south and in May of 1864, they joined the Atlanta Campaign. On July 22, 1864, as they moved toward Atlanta the fighting could be heard and the fighting continued to be heard as they marched on into the line of battle and they were ordered to fire. It was then that S.W. lost his good friend, as Private Wiser fell to the ground before him. It was S.W. who sent the news home to Betsy and the rest of the family.

Betsy was always so overjoyed to receive letters from Private Wiser as she was that summer morning when she stopped at the post office to inquire about the mail. Betsy sat on the front porch steps of the little Franconia Post Office and hurriedly opened the letter as Adaline lingered inside talking to some of their neighbors. It didn't take long for Betsy to read the fateful news of her husband's death and her joy instantaneously turned to uncontrollable weeping. Adaline rushed to be at Betsy's side, sitting down beside her on the steps. Adaline put her arms around her sister and hugged her tightly as the tears streamed down their faces. Their neighbors who were also at the post office offered their condolences and gave the young women a ride home.

Mrs. Truby was on the front porch when they arrived home and she knew something was terribly wrong before they even set foot on the porch.

"Oh, please Lord, spare us the news of yet another death," she silently prayed.

The neighbors kindly offered to ride into Kalida to inform Private Wiser's next of kin of his death. Betsy had told them about the letter on the ride home.

"Oh, Miss Betsy, would you like for us to stop at the preacher's house? We can ask him to drive out this way," offered the woman.

"That would be most kind of ye," answered Betsy. "And thank ye for the ride home."

"No trouble at all. We'll drop back by tomorrow and see if you'll be needing anything. We're mighty sorry for your loss," the couple said before they drove away.

Betsy had lost the love of her life, the only love she had ever known. She was married in March and a widow in July.

Betsy found no solace when her mother encouraged her to apply for the widow's military pension. Betsy found excuses not to attend church as she intensely labored doing the farm chores and keeping house to settle her mind.

Adaline continued to receive letters from S.W. although the letters were few and slow coming. Betsy no longer visited the post office with Adaline and Adaline found herself missing the old Betsy and the joy they once shared as sisters. Adaline continued with her prayer vigil and held on to the hope of a higher power and precious thoughts of her beloved.

Sherman's March to the Sea

On November 15, 1864, the 57th Ohio Regiment joined General Sherman's March to the Sea. By December 21st of 1864 the Union occupied Savanah, Georgia. S.W. once again missed spending Christmas with the family and Adaline was worried after not receiving any letters for such a long time. It was much later and after the new year before Adaline received a letter. Adaline was so hoping it would be good news, that S.W. might tell her the war was coming to an end and he would be home soon. As always S.W. told her how much he loved her and he always asked about the family. Adaline had been looking forward to news or even speculation of the war ending.

"Mama, this letter tis not very promising. I am fearful that

S.W. shan't return. Oh, what shall I do if I receive dreadful news?" Adaline sat at the table sobbing.

"My daughter, ye must continue to have faith," said Mrs. Truby as she sat down at the table with Adaline.

"Faith! What good is faith? Samuel and my husband are dead! And young Gilbert lay dead somewhere in a grave in Kentucky! I shan't stand here and listen to ye speak of faith!" Betsy screamed out at her Mama before running out the front door to be alone.

"Mama, she doesn't mean what she says. Ye know she is still grieving. She was so in love with Private Wiser." Adaline smiled at her Mama and reached out to hold her hand to comfort her.

"I know Betsy is grieving. I shall pray for her," replied Mrs. Truby.

Later that afternoon Adaline visited with Aunt Sarah and Amy Ann. While she visited them she composed a letter to S.W. telling him of all the latest local news.

My Dearest S.W.,

I am visiting with Aunt Sarah and Amy Ann today. I shall tell ye of all the latest news and reports that might be of interest to ye. The farmers are now paid a high price for corn, wheat, and oats. The highest prices of all time are being paid for lamb's wool and fur. Maybe we should raise sheep when ye get home? The fur dealers 'round here are happy 'bout the prices too. There be a new boot, shoe, and saddle shop in town now. It be called the Hide and Leather Shop. Mrs. Gordon has opened a new dress and cloak shop. She has the latest fashions and children's clothing. Aunt Sarah and Amy Ann visit there often. Mr. McClure is a bit upset over the new saloon and grocery that just opened. They be selling every kind of liquor and of good quality. Folks say they keep plenty stock of sugar and coffee. I shan't see how they keep a constant stock. Amy Ann tells me the lemonade is mighty good there. I wouldn't know 'bout it. Mama still does business at McClure's. I hope this terrible war is almost over. I do miss ye so. Please write as often as ye can.

I send ye all my love,
Adaline

Sherman's Carolinas Campaign

It was early March when the 57th arrived in North Carolina. On March 12th of 1865, S.W. and several other soldiers were captured by the enemy as they entered Fayetteville,

North Carolina. A Confederate Calvary rapidly approached the small group of Union Soldiers as they were following orders to breakup and surround the city. Fighting broke out, shots were fired and a small group of Union soldiers were captured. S.W. was among the group as the Confederates took their weapons and bound the hands of the Union soldiers.

It was on the banks of the Cape Fear River where the Confederate Officer ordered all the Union soldiers to be lined up, shot and thrown into the river. The young intoxicated Confederate officer loudly gave the order to kill them all. Only after watching some of the men fall to their death, he ordered the killing to be stopped. The young Officer hung his head in despair and wept. S.W.'s life had been spared.

S.W. traveled over four hundred miles as a prisoner-of-war, traveling south along the way to Andersonville Prison. S.W was declared absent from the military from March through April as his whereabouts were unknown. On April 9th,1865, General Robert E. Lee surrendered his army making this date the official end to the Civil War but fighting continued in the South as news of his surrender was slow to reach many southern areas.

On May 14th, 1865, S.W. was a paroled prisoner and sent to the College Green Barracks in Maryland which served as a hospital and barracks for the Northern troops. S.W. arrived back at Camp Chase on May 20th of 1865.

Five months had gone by since Adaline received S.W.'s last letter and it had been over a year since last she saw him. She and the family waited in fear to hear of any news or reports. Even Miss Lily desperately tried to obtain information and to get word to him that the family was most worried. And when they heard not a single reply from him or the military they began to fear the worst.

It was almost midnight in late May when someone came knocking at the front door of the Truby's farm house. The dogs commenced to barking at the ragged and half-starved man with tattered shoes and sore feet. The strangers' hair was unkempt and his face unshaven. Mrs. Truby called out to question who the caller might be.

"It is S.W. and I've come home." The feeble voice answered.

Mrs. Truby unlatched the door and Adaline followed her with a lantern to shine on the man who claimed to be S.W. but the stranger didn't look like or even sound like the S.W. they knew. Inadequate nutrition and exposure to the elements had taken a toll on the young soldier who stood on the porch and was so weakened he could barely speak. Adaline looked in disbelief at his hollow eyes and sunken face as he could only speak a little above a whisper.

"Adaline, I've come home," S.W. managed to respond.

"Oh, S.W.! I thought I shan't ever lay eyes on ye again."

Adaline put her arms around him and hugged him. Mrs. Truby and Adaline assisted him into the house as they quickly discovered how weakened he was. "S.W. come in and have a bite to eat!" Betsy offered as she rushed to get him a chair. "Would ye like some bread puddin'?" Betsy asked with a twinkle in her eye.

"That sounds mighty good," uttered S.W. through dry parched lips. It had been a long awaited homecoming and now Adaline and S.W. were finally together.

Epilogue

After the war was over S.W., also known as Sylvester Wilson Jeffrey, and who sometimes referred to himself as Wilson, journeyed home to be with his wife, Adaline. He continued his life as a farmer living in Putnam County, Ohio. S.W. and Adaline enjoyed a large family of eight children. Mrs. Truby made her home with the young couple and continued living with them for many years. The hope is that Betsy remarried, however no additional records have been located regarding her. Charlotte did get married and remained in Putnam County. Oliver also married and lived in Paulding County. Amy Ann left a dead-end trail as no more records could be found of her. Gilbert died in the war as did Samuel and Private Wiser. S.W.'s life was spared during the Civil War as told to me by my grandmother, who was S.W.'s daughter. S.W. was in the 57th Ohio Regiment, Company A, from Putnam County. Accounts of his travels were taken from military records. All other characters and events are a figment of the writer's imagination, except for historical events and places. We can only imagine that Henry was reunited with his family after the war.

I hope you enjoyed going back in time and all the characters who made this story come to life.

L.E. Hutchinson

Photos and Documents

Putnam County, Ohio, Courthouse
names of all veterans engraved on the walls.

Roster of Ohio Soldiers 1861-66.

State of Ohio
Adjutant General's Department
Columbus, 1887

OFFICIAL ROSTER

OF THE

SOLDIERS OF THE STATE OF OHIO

IN THE

WAR OF THE REBELLION,

1861—1866.

VOL. V.

54TH–69TH REGIMENTS—INFANTRY.

COMPILED UNDER DIRECTION OF THE ROSTER COMMISSION:

JOSEPH B. FORAKER, GOVERNOR,   JAMES. S. ROBINSON, SEC'Y OF STATE
H. A. AXLINE, ADJUTANT-GENERAL.

PUBLISHED BY AUTHORITY OF THE GENERAL ASSEMBLY.

AKRON, O. :
THE WERNER PTG. AND MFG. CO.
1887.

Official Roster
Soldiers of the State of Ohio 1861-1866

Names.	Rank.	Age	Date of Entering the Service	Period of Service	Remarks.
Collar, Henry	Private	22	Sept. 2, 1861	3 yrs.	Mustered out Sept. 12, 1864, at East Point, Ga., on expiration of term of service.
Cox, William	do	21	Feb. 14, 1864	3 yrs.	Mustered out with company Aug. 14, 1865.
Critton, James	do	20	Sept. 2, 1861	3 yrs.	Died March 20, 1862, at Cincinnati, O.
Crider, Jacob	do	33	Jan. 4, 1864	3 yrs.	Discharged Sept. 26, 1864, at East Point, Ga., on Surgeon's certificate of disability.
Christ, John	do	25	Sept. 2, 1861	3 yrs.	Mustered out Sept. 12, 1864, at East Point, Ga., on expiration of term of service.
Dalzell, Robert	do	24	Sept. 2, 1861	3 yrs.	Discharged June 20, 1862, at hospital, St. Louis, Mo., on Surgeon's certificate of disability.
Degarmo, James	do	45	Oct. 1, 1861	3 yrs.	Died June 26, 1862, at Corinth, Miss.
Dicus, Jacob N	do	29	Jan. 4, 1864	3 yrs.	Mustered out with company Aug. 14, 1865.
Dickey, Daniel D	do	24	Sept. 2, 1861	3 yrs.	Discharged July 31, 1862, at hospital, Columbus, O., on Surgeon's certificate of disability.
Discher, John	do	29	Sept. 2, 1861	3 yrs.	Mustered out with company Aug. 14, 1865; veteran.
Elston, John	do	21	Feb. 29, 1864	3 yrs.	Wounded July 22, 1864, in battle of Atlanta, Ga.; absent in General Hospital at Camp Dennison, O.; discharged April 17, 1865, on Surgeon's certificate of disability.
Evans, John	do	26	Sept. 2, 1861	3 yrs.	Mustered out Sept. 12, 1864, at East Point, Ga., on expiration of term of service.
Ford, Benjamin F	do	20	Jan. 26, 1864	3 yrs.	Mustered out with company Aug. 14, 1865.
Foster, Robert	do	21	Sept. 2, 1861	3 yrs.	Reduced from Corporal ——; died March 17, 1865, at Wilmington, N. C.; veteran.
Frazie, Daniel W	do	18	Sept. 2, 1861	3 yrs.	Discharged June 20, 1862, at hospital, Columbus, O., on Surgeon's certificate of disability.
Freiberger, Joseph F. S	do	21	Sept. 2, 1861	3 yrs.	Mustered out Sept. 12, 1864, at East Point, Ga., on expiration of term of service.
Furguson, Martin	do	27	Sept. 2, 1861	3 yrs.	Died May 18, 1862, at Evansville, Ind.
Garner, George S	do	37	Jan. 29, 1864	3 yrs.	Died April 13, 1865, at Newbern, N. C.
Geyer, Orville W	do	19	Jan. 29, 1864	3 yrs.	Mustered out July 12, 1865, at Little Rock, Ark., by order of War Department; veteran.
Gillett, Milton G	do	22	Sept. 17, 1864	3 yrs.	Mustered out May 30, 1865, at Columbus, O., by order of War Department.
Good, Andrew J	do	18	Jan. 27, 1864	3 yrs.	Absent, sick in General Hospital at Portsmouth Grove, R. I.; discharged July 31, 1865, on Surgeon's certificate of disability.
Good, George W	do	20	Jan. 27, 1864	3 yrs.	Died July 18, 1864, at Marietta, Ga.
Groves, Nathan	do	18	Feb. 29, 1864	3 yrs.	Died June 25, 1864, at Marietta, Ga.
Guffy, Joseph	do	22	Sept. 2, 1861	3 yrs.	Discharged Aug. 6, 1862, at hospital, Columbus, O., on Surgeon's certificate of disability.
Hart, William	do	18	Feb. 24, 1864	3 yrs.	Mustered out with company Aug. 14, 1865.
Harris, Jacob	do	18	Sept. 2, 1861	3 yrs.	Died April 3, 1862, at Shiloh, Tenn.
Harris, Isaac	do	19	Sept. 2, 1861	3 yrs.	Killed April 6, 1862, at battle of Shiloh, Tenn.
Harris, Abraham	do	22	Feb. 6, 1864	3 yrs.	Killed July 22, 1864, in battle of Atlanta, Ga.
Harris, Thaddeus	do	19	Sept. 2, 1861	3 yrs.	
Harris, Arthur	do	21	Sept. 2, 1861	3 yrs.	Discharged Jan. 19, 1862, at hospital, Columbus, O., on Surgeon's certificate of disability.
Harris, Simon P	do	28	Sept. 2, 1861	3 yrs.	Mustered out June 16, 1865, at Louisville, Ky., on expiration of term of sevice.
Harman, George C	do	27	Sept. 2, 1861	3 yrs.	Mustered out June 16, 1865, at Louisville, Ky., on expiration of term of service.
Hardy, John	do	30	Feb. 14, 1864	3 yrs.	
Hayden, Andrew	do	42	Jan. 26, 1864	3 yrs.	Absent, sick in General Hospital July 28, 1864; no further record found.
Hayden, Nathaniel	do	18	Feb. 8, 1864	3 yrs.	Died Jan. 6, 1865.
Hendricks, William B	do	25	Aug. 26, 1862	3 yrs.	
Higit, Isaac Q	do	21	Jan. 4, 1864	3 yrs.	Died March 10, 1864.
Hoffer, Andrew	do	19	Sept. 2, 1861	3 yrs.	Died June 16, 1862, at Camp Dennison, O.
Hollabaugh, George	do	32	Sept. 2, 1861	3 yrs.	Died Nov. 8, 1862.
Holcomb, Cyrus L	do	31	Sept. 2, 1861	3 yrs.	Wounded June 27, 1864, at battle of Kenesaw Mountain, Ga.; absent in General Hospital; transferred to Co. B, 6th Regiment Veteran Reserve Corps; discharged Aug. 24, 1865, on Surgeon's certificate of disability; veteran.
Horn, Washington	do	19	Feb. 29, 1864	3 yrs.	Mustered out with company Aug. 14, 1865.
House, George	do	42	Jan. 4, 1864	3 yrs.	Mustered out with company Aug. 14, 1865.
Jeffry, Sylvester	do	20	Sept. 2, 1861	3 yrs.	Mustered out June 12, 1865, at Camp Chase, O., by order of War Department; veteran.
Johnson, Nathaniel	do	45	Sept. 2, 1861	3 yrs.	
Jones, John	do	20	Sept. 2, 1861	3 yrs.	Mustered out with company Aug. 14, 1865; veteran.
Kennedy, William	do	24	Sept. 15, 1861	3 yrs.	Died July 23, 1864, of wounds received same day in action near Atlanta, Ga.; veteran.
Ladd, Joel	do	19	Jan. 4, 1864	3 yrs.	Died May ——, 1864, at Marietta, Ga.
Lane, Thomas U	do	23	Sept. 2, 1861	3 yrs.	Died July 17, 1863, at Memphis, Tenn.
Loub, Leratus	do	18	Jan. 27, 1864	3 yrs.	Mustered out with company Aug. 14, 1865.
Ludlow, Andrew	do	22	Sept. 2, 1861	3 yrs.	Died April 8, 1863, at Memphis, Tenn.
Martin, James K. P	do	20	Sept. 15, 1861	3 yrs.	Killed July 22, 1864, in battle of Atlanta, Ga.; veteran.

Official Roster Soldiers of the State of Ohio

FIFTY-SEVENTH REGIMENT OHIO VOLUNTEER INFANTRY.

THREE YEARS' SERVICE.

THIS Regiment was organized at Camp Dennison, Ohio, in October, 1861, to serve three years. The original members (except veterans) were mustered out by detachments in November, 1864, and the organization, composed of veterans and recruits, retained in service until August 15, 1865, when it was mustered out in accordance with orders from the War Department.

Only a partial official list of battles, in which this Regiment bore an honorable part, has yet been published by the War Department, but the following list has been compiled, after careful research, during the preparation of this work:

SHILOH, TENN.,	APRIL 6–7, 1862.
MORNING SUN, TENN.,	JULY 1, 1862.
WOLF CREEK BRIDGE, MISS.,	SEPTEMBER 23, 1862.
CHICKASAW BAYOU, MISS.,	DECEMBER 28–29, 1862.
ARKANSAS POST, ARK.,	JANUARY 11, 1863.
VICKSBURG, MISS. (Siege of and Assaults),	MAY 18 to JULY 4, 1863.
JACKSON, MISS.,	JULY 9–16, 1863.
MISSION'RIDGE, TENN.,	NOVEMBER 25, 1863.
SNAKE CREEK GAP, GA.,	MAY 8, 1864.
RESACA, GA.,	MAY 13–16, 1864.
DALLAS, GA.,	MAY 25 to JUNE 4, 1864.
KENESAW MOUNTAIN, GA.,	JUNE 9–30, 1864.
ATLANTA, GA. (Hood's First Sortie),	JULY 22, 1864.
ATLANTA, GA. (Siege of),	JULY 28 to SEPTEMBER 2, 1864.
JONESBORO, GA.,	AUGUST 31 to SEPTEMBER 1, 1864.
STATESBORO, GA.,	DECEMBER 4, 1864.
FORT McALLISTER, GA.,	DECEMBER 13, 1864.
FAYETTEVILLE, N. C.,	MARCH 13, 1865.
BENTONVILLE, N. C.,	MARCH 19–21, 1865.

(127)

Official Roster Soldiers of the State of Ohio

Sylvester Wilson Jeffrey

Sigler Cemetery, Putnam County, Ohio

S.W. Jeffrey's Civil War Pension Records. "Disabled by inflammation of the stomach, and injuries of the wrist and elbow, at Fayetteville, N.C., March 13, 1865, the results of ill-treatment and exposure while a prisoner of war."

STATE OF _____ COUNTY OF _____

Sworn to and subscribed before me this day by the above-named affiant _____ and I certify that I read said affi-

_____ affiant _____ including the words _____ erased,

____ the words _____ added,

and acquainted _____ with its contents before _____ executed the same. I further certify that I am in nowise

interested in said case, nor am I concerned in its prosecution; and that said affiant _____ personally

known to me and that _____ creditable person.

[L. s.]

[Official Signature]

[Official Character.]

Page 2, Civil War Pension Records. Bureau of Pension.

General Affidavit for S.W. Jeffrey. This is a request for a military pension which S.W. applied for later in life. The latter part is written in his handwriting and his signature.

War Department Records of Sylvester W. Jeffrey. This document verifies his enlistment, travels, Fayetteville, capture, and date of discharge.

shows him Prvt mustered out with detachment
that place. Hosp Records show him treated
at July 20/63 in 2nd. Dysentery: returned to duty
July 25/63.

Prisoner of War Records show him Captured at Fayetteville,
N.C. March 12. 65. Present at Newberry S.C. April
65. Paroled at Sister Ferry or Augusta, Ga. May
65. Reported at College Green Ohio Md. May 17.
65. Sent to Camp Chase, Ohio May 17. 65. show he arrived
May 20. 1865.

The records of this Office furnish no further evidence
of disability. The records of Fayetteville N.C. are not
on file.

R. C. DRUM,
Adjutant General.

By

Page 2, War Department Records.

Adaline Jeffrey, wife of Sylvester W. Jeffrey.

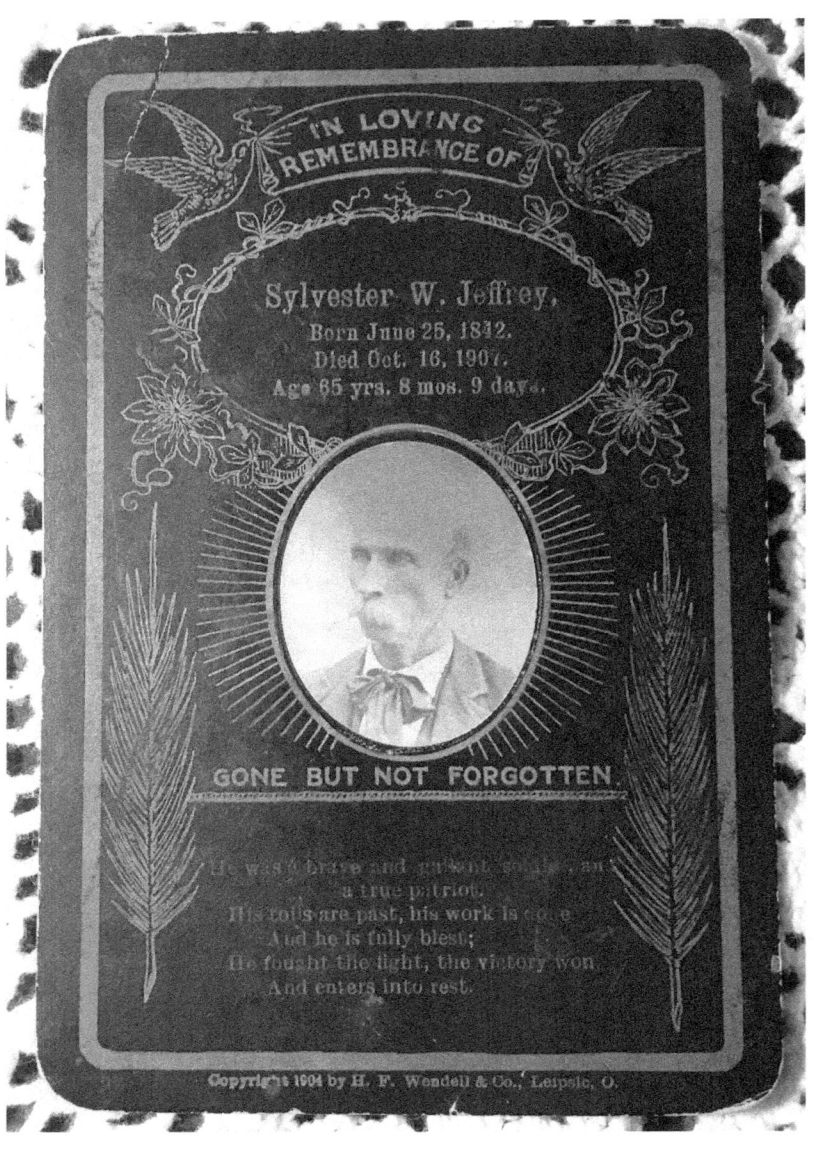

About the Author

L.E. Hutchinson grew up in the 1950's and was raised on a farm in southeastern Ohio, in the foothills of the Appalachian Mountains. Her interest in writing goes back to some intriguing stories her grandmother told about her great-grandfather, who fought in the Civil War. The stories her grandmother told aroused interest in researching the family history and historical events. Hutchinson also writes children's literature with rhyming words and verses that are geared towards teaching the alphabet.

Hutchinson has worked with the pediatric population providing Occupational Therapy in school-based and in-home settings. Presently, she is working with the geriatric population through therapeutic rehabilitation.